Gift of the Amazon

Barry & Darlene Greenawald

This book is a work of fiction. Names, characters, places, and incidents are the product of the authors' imagination or are used fictitiously. Any resemblance to actual events, locales, or persons, living or dead, is coincidental.

If you purchase this book without a cover you should be aware that this book may have been stolen property and reported as "unsold and destroyed" to the publisher. In such case neither the author nor the publisher has received any payment for this "stripped book."

DEDICATION

To animal lovers, particularly bird lovers, and animal welfare organizations, including veterinarians and humane caregivers;

All children and their families who have suffered or are suffering from childhood cancer;

Family and friends who provided valuable feedback and support to us while writing this book and;

To Cody, our first parrot, who started it all.

ACKNOWLEDGMENTS

The authors wish to acknowledge the following:

Cover design: Barry Greenawald, Katherine Edwins Schumm, and James Stueber.

Cover images: Mystic Jungle by Kanea/Shutterstock.com, Shaman by Ammit Jack/Shutterstock.com, White Dove on back cover by ifong/Shutterstock.com.

Editing: Thank you to members of the "Writers of the Villages" and the "Working Writers Workshop" in The Villages, Florida for valuable editing assistance.

Prologue

THE SNAKE STRUCK like a lightning bolt. An Indian boy, about eight years old, with red painted stripes on his face, didn't know what hit him. Grimacing in pain, he turned to see large fangs firmly embedded in the calf of his right leg. Fear penetrated the boy's entire body as he looked into the snake's piercing yellow eyes. The snake coiled its head back as if to strike again, but turned and quickly slithered away.

It was just a matter of time before the venom did its job. Breathing heavily, the child stumbled to his feet as the deadly poison pulsated up his leg. His heart raced and the burning, throbbing pain intensified. *I'm going to die.*

The boy understood what it meant to be bitten by a bushmaster, also known as the surucucu by the people of the Amazon rainforest. Many times, he had heard the men talk about this devil snake and the horrible death several in his tribe had suffered.

He shouldn't have foolishly strayed into the forbidden area to pick the bright blue berries that beckoned and urged him to wander from the safety of the trail and the hunting party that had ventured away from their village.

It was his very first hunting expedition, and he had felt so grown up when the men of the village had decided it was time for him to join them. He had carried his little bow and arrows and imitated the men knowing one day he, too, would be a great hunter and provide food and protection for the village.

Why didn't I listen to my father who warned me to stay close?

The boy trembled and could feel his strength waning. He knew he had little time, if any. From deep within, he mustered every ounce of strength he had to wrap his arms around a nearby tauari tree. He pulled himself up and hobbled toward the direction of the hunting party, screaming loud and long and piercingly.

* * *

The boy's scream interrupted everyday life in the surrounding rainforest and the usually peaceful village. Jittery howler monkeys and tamarins vaulted among the trees with the help of their prehensile tails as if escaping an unknown demon. Spider monkeys chattered, preparing their group to evacuate a dangerous situation. Birds squawked and jabbered noisily throughout the rainforest and warned the others of the presence of danger.

The hunting party of scantily clad Cinta Larga Indian men with black, bowl-shaped haircuts and large bark sashes around their waists turned in the direction of the boy's scream. Surrounding villagers, eyes fearful, halted their everyday chores of gathering wood and skinning small animals. Indian women pulling grubs from rotting palms and working gardens of plantains, corn, and cassava dropped their digging sticks and looked around with restless eyes searching for the origin of the scream. Children, who moments ago scampered about loudly playing tag, suddenly stopped.

Outside the village, a few men, who had waded into the shallows of their favorite fishing pool, jerked their heads around, bows drawn and pointed, ready to do battle with an unseen enemy.

Only a magnificent waterfall remained unaffected by the sudden chaos. The water continued to pour gracefully over a steep rocky cliff and cascade in slender energetic leaps into the pool where the men had been fishing.

These Cinta Larga Indians of Brazil lived a self-sufficient, peaceful existence with a spiritual connection to their surroundings. Although they avoided conflict, they fiercely defended their territory and way of life. Many of their small villages dotted the Brazilian landscape. Family was the most important unit of their social organization, and they were free to move from one village to another. The Cinta Largas respected nature, and they had a deep understanding of the creatures that inhabited the forest. They cherished and protected their young believing that their children were the key to a better future.

* * *

Interrupted by the piercing scream from an all too familiar voice, the boy's father turned to the others. "That was my son," he shouted. "We must find him."

After a frantic search, they found the boy alive but barely breathing. Glancing at the fang marks on the boy's leg, the father cried out, "Surucucu! Surucucu! We must call upon Ubjara. It is our only hope." He picked up his son and with help from the others quickly carried him to their village.

* * *

Ubjara, the aging Village medicine man, among the most respected of all the Cinta Largas, occupied a special place in the hearts of his people. At the age of eighty, though no longer the daring, young warrior who used to scout the jungle terrain, Ubjara had transcended to a different being.

He stood stoically at the edge of the busy village and crossed his yellowed, leathery arms. A gentle breeze blew his long, scraggly, gray hair away from his time-chiseled, wrinkled face as he gazed upward at the tall trees nearby. A white birthmark, shaped like a butterfly with a wingspan of about two inches, glistened against the dark skin on the back of his shoulder.

A rawhide bracelet with two gold charms, one in the shape of a butterfly, the other with three twisted prongs, dangled and jingled from Ubjara's wrist as he raised his arm. As if on command, a beautiful Blue-fronted Amazon parrot sprung off from a nearby tall tree branch, glided gracefully downward, and landed on his outstretched arm. Predominantly green in color, the parrot had yellow feathering around his eyes and yellow and red markings on the shoulders of his wings.

Ubjara stole a quick kiss on the bird's most outstanding feature, his striking turquoise-blue forehead, and whispered, "Come, my little one, time for you to go to work."

With the parrot on his shoulder, Ubjara entered a modest tribal hut of bamboo poles and thatched leaves, and peered down at the child, sweating and moaning as he lay on an animal skin.

Rocking back and forth, tears rolling down her cheeks, the boy's mother slumped by the youngster's side dabbing a cloth on his feverish head.

The child's eyes grew distant as they started to roll up into his forehead, a sign he was succumbing to the venom of the devil snake.

Ubjara knelt down and touched the boy's burning skin. He then raised his arm up to the parrot, who stepped onto his hand. Upon moving his arm down, the parrot settled onto the boy's shoulder. The boy's mother drew back her trembling hands and closed her eyes. The parrot turned his head toward Ubjara, who gave a slow, easy nod.

* * *

Outside the hut, dozens of villagers gathered with empty stares upon their painted faces. They lifted their hands to the heavens, gazed upward, and danced shaking their rattles of hollowed out gourds filled with stones. They chanted and sang power songs to invite good spirits to assist their great healer. Tribal members backed away and fell to their knees as a supernatural blue glow radiated from the hut.

Dusk descended upon the rainforest. Ubjara, with the parrot back on his shoulder, walked out of the hut, nodded, and quietly sauntered away as he often did after performing his magic.

* * *

At first light the following morning, Ubjara stood with arms folded by the hut along with his companion parrot. The tribal members gathered once again. With expectations mounting, they jabbered while gazing wide-eyed at Ubjara and the hut. The chatter ceased and their attention heightened as the boy's mother emerged from the hut smiling in relief. She held her son's hand steadying his shaky legs as he walked out of the hut. The child's eyes squinted against the piercing sun, but he raised his head and a hesitant smile spread across his face. After leaning forward and holding still for a moment, the tribal members, with shouts of joy and praise, raised their hands and spears, and cheered jubilantly.

"You have done well, my friend," Ubjara praised as he smiled and stroked his parrot's head. His smile gave way to a distant stare and his chin trembled as he spoke.

"Together we have saved many, but I fear this may be my last."

* * *

Several days later as the sun peeked over the horizon, Ubjara strolled along a narrow dirt path into an open field. It was unusual for him to make excursions far into the forest near the hunting and fishing grounds, but for some reason, he felt the need to be alone with nature.

Clutching his familiar braided bracelet with the two gold charms given to him so long ago, he stopped to gaze at the nearby magnificent waterfall.

The water cascaded gently from the towering cliff and roared as it entered the large pool below.

He looked up and nodded to his companion Blue-fronted Amazon parrot sitting calmly in a nearby tree. Ubjara staggered, grabbed his chest, grimaced, and collapsed to the ground.

* * *

Two other tribal members who had been fishing in the pool dropped their bows and ran to him.

One knelt, cupped his mouth with one hand, and shook his head. "He is gone." He kissed Ubjara's forehead then carefully removed the medicine man's bracelet. "We must give this to the Chief," he said with a voice cracking with emotion.

From a nearby tree branch, Ubjara's companion Amazon parrot looked down and bellowed a loud, agonizing shriek. The parrot spread his wings revealing a white butterfly-shaped birthmark—the same mark as on the back of Ubjara's shoulder. On a branch above the parrot, sat a pure white dove.

The Villagers wept as the two men carried their sacred medicine man into the village and lay him before the Chief. The tribesman knelt and placed the bracelet at the Chief's feet.

The Chief picked up the bracelet and held it high. "It is time to pass this on."

* * *

On the following day, the village Chief ordered six young tribal men to carry Ubjara's body, wrapped in animal skins, to its final resting place near the hunting and fishing grounds far from the village. The Chief, expressionless and adorned with red and green macaw feathers on his headdress and gold armlets signifying his status, led a procession of villagers past the waterfall and up a hill. At the grave site on the hilltop, hundreds of white butterflies fluttered wildly about.

The Chief, acting as if he barely noticed the strange butterflies, gazed toward the sky and sternly proclaimed:

"Our great village healer, who saved many young lives, is at the end of his journey. May a mighty tree that preserves the healing power grow from his grave. Only an ancestor of his winged companion may release the soul of our healer and the gift of healing from the tree.

8

One, not of this tribe, may carry it to a worthy young one who deserves to live to serve others. One day the healing power will come back to you again, my people."

After burying Ubjara, the natives descended from the hilltop.

Ubjara's companion Blue-fronted Amazon parrot flew by, as if giving a final salute to his old friend, and disappeared into the rainforest.

* * *

Days later, black clouds drifted across the sky, thunder boomed and lightning cracked as a shattering earthquake rumbled across the Brazilian landscape in the immediate vicinity of the burial ground. The hill with Ubjara's body creaked wide open. Explosions, falling rock, and rushing water engulfed the area. The grave site plunged deep into the earth, groaning and screeching. It rose again, higher and higher forming a steep rock face that projected straight up into the sky, gradually becoming a mountain with vertical cliffs, high above the existing waterfall. Swelling rivers roared and encircled the base of the mountain.

Far away, villagers fell to the ground. Their homes crumbled and scattered like dried leaves in the wind.

Amazingly, the earthquake ceased as quickly as it started. As dust and debris slowly cleared, the villagers looked up in awe at the newly formed distant mountain.

After an eerie silence, the loud squawk of a distant parrot echoed through the shattered rainforest. Ubjara's companion parrot managed to survive the cataclysmic event. Why was he spared? Perhaps he lived to have offspring, and his offspring to have offspring. But what did the future have in store for them? Would poachers capture these beautiful birds and take them away from their home? Perhaps their destiny would be one that no one could imagine. Perhaps, they would fulfill their purpose in life in another place, in another time, in another way.

A white dove sitting on a tree limb overlooking the now calm landscape spread its wings and took flight. Higher and higher the dove flew becoming a tiny white speck eventually dissolving into the drifting clouds across the blue sky.

Chapter 1

The Nightmare

— Spring, 2011 – East Stroudsburg, PA

DEIRDRE GARDNER THRASHED about in bed mumbling incoherently. She flailed her arms, as if swatting flies, knocking the alarm clock off the nightstand.

Her husband, Ben, jolted awake, narrowly escaping one of her unintentional jabs aimed directly at the small of his back.

Ben turned on a bedside lamp and gently shook her. "Dee ... Dee."

As she jerked her head around, Ben gently brushed locks of her long golden blond hair away from her cheeks glistening with perspiration. She whimpered, placed her hand on her head, and sighed.

Ben whispered, "Again?"

She took a deep breath and sat up. "It's almost the same darn dream every time."

"*Almost* the same? Whaddya mean? What's different?"

"I'm still in what looks like a hospital elevator. But *this* time a bird ... a green bird with a blue forehead like a parrot ... I think ... squawks and flaps its wings like it's suspended in midair, almost as if it's trying to tell me something."

"A parrot? Okay, so why in the world do you think the parrot is trying to tell you something?"

"I don't know. I can't explain it. And there's still a man in a white coat who looks like a doctor or something just staring vacantly at me like he always does without saying a word. Behind him is the same blurred image of a little girl in a hospital bed. Suddenly that green bird flaps wildly past the man's face."

"Whoa, seems to me that bird, which probably is a parrot the way you're describing it, has now become a major part of your dream."

"I guess so. It's so strange. And what's really weird is, the doctor finally speaks. He calls out, 'Just one thing will save her.' After that, the elevator doors slam shut just like they always do when the dream ends."

"Now there's a parrot in your dream and also a doctor saying, 'Just one thing will save her'? Mmm ... whaddya suppose that's all about?"

"How in the heck do I know. I'm so confused, and I can't remember the last time I had a good night's sleep because of this darn dream."

Ben cupped his hands around Deirdre's sweaty face. Her high cheekbones and childishly-round face gave her a unique cuteness any man would adore.

"Sweetheart, between writing your books and worrying about Penny, you're under too much stress. I know we talked about taking a vacation when I'm on my sabbatical this fall, but that's five months away. Maybe we should plan a little getaway before that, like this summer sometime."

"I don't know, but just listen to me a minute," Deirdre insisted as she removed Ben's hands from her face. "I know that bird is trying to tell me something, and it's driving me crazy. Maybe I should go to a shrink or something. They're supposed to be good at interpreting dreams."

"Dee, it's Penny. You've become consumed with trying to figure out some way you can help your little niece. I'm afraid her fate rests in the hands of a higher power than you or I, or anyone for that matter."

"There you go again. If God is so wonderful, why does he let cancer take the lives of such young children? And why couldn't He have given us a child? Life is just so unfair," Deirdre sighed, bursting into tears.

For several moments, Ben and Deirdre embraced each other.

Deirdre broke the silence. "I know how frustrating this is for you. But thanks for always being there for me." She kissed Ben good night and pulled the covers up around her tear-stained face. "What would I do without you?"

Of course, Ben was right, Deirdre rationalized. *But I don't know what I'd do if we lost Penny now. There must be a way to save her and I'm going to find it.*

While drifting off, Deirdre couldn't help but think how different she and Ben were. He was the steady one, the young ecology professor with a penchant for logic. He loved the outdoors and had a desire to explore exotic lands. She, on the other hand, was the impulsive one, the aspiring writer. She was the pedal-to-the-metal reckless one, always chasing a dream, and now a dream seemed to be chasing her.

* * *

A few days later, Ben leaned on his classroom desk at East Stroudsburg University, a small college nestled in the foothills of the Pocono Mountains in Pennsylvania. The name plate on the desk read, Ben Gardner, Ph.D. Rubbing his fingers through his neatly-trimmed beard, he browsed through the latest edition of the *Journal of Ecology and Environmental Sciences* while waiting for students to complete their final exams.

One by one, students dropped their completed test papers onto Ben's desk and walked out of the classroom. Sabio, a brown-skinned student with long black hair, and the last to drop off his exam, stopped next to Ben's desk.

"Yes, Sabio?" Ben asked.

Sabio raised his hand to his face and rubbed his chin. "Professor Gardner, you, as they say, hit the head of the nail about the rainforests."

"Thanks, Sabio. You mean I hit the nail on the head. By the way, I've been meaning to tell you, I'm thinking about taking a trip to your homeland in a few months when I'm on sabbatical."

Sabio tilted his head and moved slightly closer to Ben. "Really? Cool. How come?"

"Got a seat on a commission to investigate logging and mining operations in the rainforest. Thought Brazil might be a good place to learn more about it. Like I said in my lecture last week, the damage that some of these companies are doing there is shameful. Loggers cut down rainforest trees for timber."

"And the miners cut down trees, too."

"You're right, Sabio. Mining operations clear entire forest areas to build roads and dig mines. If this plundering continues at the current rate, critical habitats could disappear from the planet completely within the next hundred years."

"Yes, this is true, Professor. My family there say the people are suffering. They find it harder and harder to find food to eat and are being forced off their lands. Many of my ancestors have died fighting to keep their land. Animals are losing their habitats. Birds don't have places to nest anymore."

As Sabio started toward the door, he stopped, turned, and rubbed his hand at the middle of his forehead. "Professor Gardner, if you go to Brazil, you might learn more than you think. The rainforest holds many secrets." Without saying another word, Sabio turned and continued toward the door.

"Have a good summer, Sabio," Ben yelled as Sabio walked out the door. *Hmm, I wonder what Sabio meant by many secrets.* After gathering up his papers and stuffing them into his briefcase, he headed for the school parking lot.

On the way, a whiff of chlorine in the air and children splashing and playing at a nearby backyard pool distracted him. He felt that familiar nauseating feeling as he gripped the door handle of his truck. *Shake it off, Ben, you're not in the pool. Think of Deirdre and Cody ... anything.*

Dazed, Ben grabbed the door handle to steady himself, shook his head, and climbed into his Toyota 4-Runner. After assuring himself that he was fine, he drove off and headed for home.

Chapter 2

A Little Disagreement

BEN SLAMMED ON the brakes as he drove over the small bridge guarded by gargoyle statues. After allowing time for a gray squirrel to spring out of his path to safety, he continued up the long, winding driveway, lined by tulip poplar trees, to his stone-faced, A-frame style home.

Proud of his house, Ben had worked closely with the contractor to ensure it provided an open and airy living space for Deirdre. He insisted that large glass windows and sliding glass doors encompass the front of the house. A redwood deck bordered the entire front length of the house overlooking the front yard with multiple levels of terraced landscaping sloping down to a tiny brook that babbled through the width of the well-maintained property. A leafy Wisteria vine knitted its way through the rail of the deck concealing the outdoor furniture and many potted plants resting on the deck.

Ben parked his truck under a tall poplar tree near the front of the house. Gazing over the deck railing, he saw Deirdre puttering around on the deck wearing her favorite T-shirt, the one her sister Judy had given her, with the slogan, Standing Strong Against Childhood Cancer. He felt a rush of warmth as he caught a glimpse of her youthful legs protruding from washed-out denim shorts despite the winter chill still lingering in the air.

No matter how disheveled Deirdre appeared, Ben found her attractive, downright alluring at times. Time had been good to her. Even though now in her forties, to him, she didn't look all that much different from when they first met in college years ago.

* * *

Normally this time of day, Deirdre would bang away on her laptop working on one of her books. On this day, however, she had news she couldn't wait to share with Ben, so she lingered on the deck waiting for him to arrive home from the university. She passed the time trimming the sprawling wisteria and watering flower boxes full of newly planted spring flowers, occasionally stretching her neck over the railing to be on the lookout for his 4-Runner.

Spotting Ben under the tree, she waved hello. While picking up a small bowl from the deck used for feeding an occasional visiting feral cat, a crow *cawed* loudly and swooped down close to her head. She yelped, dropped the watering can and the bowl, and scampered into the house as fast as her slender legs could carry her. *Darn birds.*

Once inside, she brushed some dirt off her clothes. While waiting for Ben to come inside, she ran to her favorite spot in the sun room, a tiny desk by a window giving her a great view of the front yard. She grabbed a letter from her desk, ran to the main living area, held the letter behind her back, and waited for Ben to enter.

Moments later, Ben walked up the small ramp to the deck and through the front door leading to the living area.

In her typical animated fashion, Deirdre rushed to him, smacked a kiss on his cheek above his dark beard, and stood there almost breathless, bouncing on her toes.

"Ooo-kay," Ben said with trepidation in his voice.

After staring at him for a moment with a fluttery feeling in her stomach, she pushed the letter in his face.

"Whoa, what's this?"

"Look at the letterhead, Child Smile Publishing. It's a letter from my publisher. Not only is he interested in my new book, but he wants me to come to New York later this year."

"New York?"

"Yeah, he wants to talk about writing a whole series of children's books. Aren't you proud of me? There's also a book fair there this fall that he would like me to go to, so he thinks that would be a good time to meet with him. What a great opportunity for us."

Ben reached out, held her by the waist and smiled widely. "Omigosh, that's fantastic. Us?"

Deirdre's heart pounded with excitement. "Remember, you said something about taking a vacation while on sabbatical. How about a nice trip to New York together?"

Ben stepped back, and rubbed his neck.

Words flowed nonstop out of Deirdre's mouth as she spoke without taking a breath. "You and I could tour the city, go to shows ... whaddya think?"

"Well, maybe."

The sudden squawk of a parrot provided a welcomed distraction.

Ben turned and sauntered into the sunroom leaving Deirdre standing with her hands on her hips. He approached a bird cage where Cody, a Yellow-collared mini Macaw, perched, wings quivering, vying for attention. Ben opened the cage door, and Cody hopped onto his outstretched hand. "Hey, Cody, what's the matter, Guy?" He then walked back to the living area and set Cody onto a small portable perch made of PVC pipe. Ben had built this perch to give Cody a place to sit in other areas of the house.

"You and that silly bird," Deirdre said with a huff. "And excuse me! Maybe?"

"Well, I can't investigate rainforest logging and mining operations very well without actually being there, now can I? And I was kinda thinking—"

Deirdre felt her body tense up as she stamped her foot down. "What? You know how much this trip to New York would mean to me. I'm already second fiddle to a stupid bird. Now loggers and miners in the jungle are more important?"

"Of course not, but New York?" He reached out, brushed his hand across her cheek, and spoke with a soft voice. "I was planning on surprising you by asking you to go to Brazil with me this fall. I can pretty much pick whatever part of Brazil I want. It just has to be an area where logging and mining is actually going on ... that's all. I thought I'd pick an area that would make a nice vacation for us too. I'm really happy about you and your book, but now this sort of messes everything up."

"That does sound kinda like fun," she said. "But can't we do something that *I* wanna do for a change?"

"Oh, sweetheart, of course we can, but I already promised the commission I would go to Brazil."

Glancing at Cody, Ben went on, "Wait, whaddya mean stupid bird?" He reached out and grabbed a photo of a Fischer's lovebird from a bookcase shelf and held it up to Deirdre's face. "Was Timmy a stupid bird too? He adored you."

"You know how I feel about birds. After all, you're afraid of water, but I wouldn't dare force you to go swimming. And you're changing the subject."

"That's different. Did you ever almost lose your life because of a bird? I don't think so. And now *you're* changing the subject. Is it because of that scary parrot you saw in your dream?"

"Of course not. The parrot isn't scary. It's just that I think that parrot in the dream is trying to tell me something."

"Maybe it's trying to tell you to go to Brazil with me."

Deirdre rubbed her hand across her forehead contemplating jungle scenarios. "Alligators, snakes and weird flying creatures. Sounds delightful. You go to Brazil, I'm going to New York."

"Weird flying creatures? You don't mean parrots, do you?"

Deirdre strolled to the kitchen and poured herself a glass of white wine. After pushing her hair out of her face, she took a sip and set the glass down. "Gee, I ... I'm not sure what I mean." Grabbing the photograph of Timmy from Ben, her voice softened. "He was kinda cute, wasn't he? I always did like that little, bright red beak of his. And at least he gave me somebody to talk to when you weren't around."

Ben rubbed his temple and put his arms around Deirdre. "You're right. Maybe dragging you to Brazil is a dumb idea. Besides, I *am* worried about your nightmares. A bird, an elevator ... mmm, those are things you fear. Let's face it—"

"And a doctor, and I think Penny too," Deirdre added.

"You're so afraid Penny's not gonna get better, and she *is* like a daughter to us. Maybe you dreamed that Penny was going to heaven."

Unable to settle herself in one place, Deirdre ran her hand through her hair and paced. "Yeah, right, like I really believe there is a heaven," she said rolling her eyes and folding her arms defiantly.

"How do you know there isn't?"

"And how do you know there is?"

"Alright, alright, I know you have your doubts, but let's not get into one of those discussions again." Scratching his head, Ben suggested, "Hey, I know—why can't we do both?"

"I don't know if we will have time for both. I was sort of thinking it would be nice to stay in New York long enough to make the trip more worthwhile. I could meet with my publisher, go to the book fair, and we could stay awhile to see the sites ... you know, make it our vacation too. Sort of like killing two birds with one stone."

"Heh, you really *do* dislike birds, don't you? Just kidding, dear. I know, how 'bout I cut my trip to Brazil short, to just a week or so. As soon as I get back, I'll join you in New York, and we'll have a nice romantic time together."

Deirdre gave Ben a lingering touch with her shoulder and smiled at him as she leaned in and lowered her voice, "As long as some sexy Chiquita Banana doesn't get her hands on you and keep you down there."

Feigning interest, he glanced up with a slow smile. "Mmmm, that is a possibility."

Deirdre whacked him on the shoulder. They laughed together, then hugged and gave each other playful kisses.

"It doesn't matter to me if you believe in heaven or not. Being with you, my dear, is heavenly, and I think you're the prettiest girl on earth," Ben said, nuzzling Deirdre's cheek.

"I wanna make sure you keep thinking that way, so tomorrow I have an appointment to get my hair done."

* * *

On the following day, Ben sat at the wheel of his Toyota 4-Runner parked in front of a building with a sign that read, Hair Express. Deirdre climbed into the car.

Ben gave her the once over. "Well, look at you."

She gazed into the visor mirror and fussed with her hair. "Looks pretty good, huh?"

"No, looks beautiful. Hope you don't mind. I have to make a quick stop at Woody's. Cody's low on food."

"If you must, you must. A place that breeds and sells those big birds with beaks like can openers is not exactly my favorite place to visit. But I know, I know … Cody needs food."

Chapter 3

Surprise Package

A SHINGLE ABOVE a small, modest building read, Woody's Bird Farm, a pet shop specializing in the breeding and sale of companion birds. The main part of the building housed the sales area with food and toys in the front and live birds toward the rear. Another room in the back, contained the nursery, breeding and general work areas. A glass observation window allowed customers in the sales area to view baby birds in the nursery directly on the other side.

In the back room, a heap of tin and ceramic feeding bowls cluttered a porcelain sink waiting to be washed.

While putting on her apron, Sylvia limped with her cane over to one side of the room. Gazing through a window to the outside, a tiny speck in the blue sky caught her attention. Mesmerized by the seemingly insignificant moving object, she watched as it grew in size until it appeared visible as a white dove, wings softly flapping.

The dove settled on a branch among yellowish-green blossoms of an oak tree along the shop's parking area.

Pushing her glasses up, Sylvia found herself fixating her thoughts on the dove for a moment, but couldn't figure out why. Scratching the side of her head, she limped back toward the sink area.

On a table, not far from the sink, sat several small incubators, each containing tiny bird eggs awaiting their turn to come to life. In one of the incubators, a single egg quivered. It rolled a little to the left, followed by a roll to the right like it couldn't decide exactly where it wanted to be. After a while, a crack, barely visible at first, appeared in the shell. Soon a small hole came into view as the tiny point of a beak emerged. It wasn't long before the entire beak poked through the shell struggling to make the hole bigger. It stopped moving as if resting for a moment. With an unexpected burst of energy, the egg cracked wide open and out tumbled a helpless parrot chick.

The hatchling, naked except for a few thin, wispy down feathers, lay still taking rapid breaths after the task of freeing itself from the egg. Blind at birth, bubble-like bluish membranes covered and protected its eyes. The beak it had so skillfully used to break through the shell and enter into this world stood out as the only feature distinguishing the hatchling as a parrot.

* * *

An air of chaos filled the breeding area of the back room. A pair of Blue and Gold Macaws squawked loudly from inside a large cage. Clang and clatter rang across the room where Amazon parrots, hanging upside down in their cages, whacked at bells with their beaks.

Smaller parrots chattered, crunched on food, and wrestled with toys hanging like tiny chandeliers in their cages.

Woody ran his fingers through his thinning hair. He turned his attention to a lonesome looking and somewhat scruffy-feathered adult Blue-fronted Amazon parrot perched quietly in a cage. Woody leaned over and cocked his head to take a closer look at the forlorn bird.

The parrot gazed back as if was thinking, *What's your problem, bud?*

Woody shook his head in disgust. "You and that damned flea market," he yelled across the room at Sylvia in his usual, gruff voice. "I still think it was a bad idea to buy this bird."

Sylvia turned and glowered at her husband. Her bad knee didn't seem to bother her as she made her way across the room moving faster than usual, cane in hand. "Oh, knock it off, you old buzzard. He looked so sad, I couldn't imagine anybody else giving Zekie a home."

Woody glared at the bird and crossed his arms. "No leg band. A poached bird I'd say."

Sylvia blew out a noisy breath. "He's an Amazon, and he was in a tiny canary cage for God's sake. And the blood test showed he's a male so I figured he'd make a good breeder."

"I'd like to have a little say in what birds we bring in here to use as breeders, too, ya know. It would be nice to have a little bit of knowledge about their background."

"All I know is … I was right. They mated, didn't they? Katie took to him right away. Her hormones kicked in the minute she saw him. She nuzzled up to Zekie like a starry-eyed teenager. And think about it … how many other male Blue fronts did we try to get her to mate with? She didn't want anything to do with them."

Woody glanced over at Katie, a female Blue-fronted Amazon parrot relaxing in her cage and preening the green down feathers under her wing. One would almost swear she had a smile on her face. He then looked over at Sylvia. "Yeah, that's something *we* haven't done in a while."

"Heh, maybe Zekie can give you some pointers."

Woody faked a grin. "Gosh, at least Katie was born in this country … not wild-caught." As Sylvia thumped toward the breeding area, Woody bellowed, "We know nothing about that vagabond you brought home. Katie only laid one stink'n egg."

In the breeding area, Sylvia peered down at the newly hatched chick. "Well, guess what, mister crank bag. Our vagabond from the flea market is a daddy. C'mere and take a look."

Woody, slipping on thick glasses, shuffled over to the incubator. On his way, he stopped and glanced out the window at the white dove sitting in the tree before peering down at the chick. "I'll be a monkey's uncle."

"You mean a parrot's uncle, don't you?"

Squinting to take a closer look, he reached for a magnifying glass. "The important thing is, we'll have a little Blue-front to sell in a few months—assuming he's healthy."

Woody inspected the newborn through the magnifying glass.

From the chick's point of view, Woody's eye must have appeared like a gigantic, gawking eyeball hovering over him like a monstrous air balloon.

Woody called out, "Hey, old lady, take a look at this."

Grabbing the magnifying glass, Sylvia peered down. "Mmm, very strange. Never saw anything like it. Aah, it's just some sorta birthmark, that's all."

Woody snatched the magnifying glass back from Sylvia and continued examining the baby bird. "Yeah, but it's pure white and—" Scratching his head, Woody gazed out the window again at the white dove. He couldn't figure out why, but for some reason he felt enchanted by the dove, as if it was watching over an event. Turning his attention back to the newborn, he waved Sylvia over. "Hey, ya know what?"

"What is it?"

"Oh, nothing, just my imagination."

"Huh, what imagination?"

"I imagine I still have hormones that can kick in too ... if you nuzzle up to me."

Sylvia waved him off. "Oh, go on, you old fart."

They chuckled together.

A parrot in a nearby cage squawked loudly as if adding his own two cents.

* * *

Gazing out the window of Ben's truck as it pulled into Woody's parking lot, the white dove in the oak tree attracted Deirdre's eye. While walking down the path leading to the front door, she stopped and stared into the tree for a moment, captivated by the dove.

Once inside, Deirdre lingered near the door and forced a smile while watching Ben examine bird food packages.

Ben picked up a bag from among many kinds of packaged bird food that lined two main aisles of the shop.

Shiny new bird cages of various sizes lined one side of the room, and hundreds of colorful birdie toys dangled along a wall. In the back area of the sales area, many species of birds in cages squawked and chirped ... parakeets, conures, macaws, and various Amazon parrots.

Woody sauntered through the door from the breeding area and approached Ben. "Howdy, Professor. Just got some new toys in that Cody might like." He waved to Deirdre. "Hi, Mrs. Gardner."

Offering a polite smile, Deirdre waved back.

Ben struggled to hold up a large bag of parrot food. "Oh, thanks, Woody. Just need some more food for now. This oughta hold Cody over for a few months.

Say, what's wrong with you? Ya look like you just saw a ghost."

"I may have. Just kidding. Actually, a new hatchling just broke out of his shell ... a little Blue-fronted Amazon parrot."

"Really? Can I see him, or her?"

"I can't take you back there. He's still in the incubator. But you can look at the little guy through the window over there. Sylvia just moved him to the viewing area."

As Ben followed Woody to the viewing window, Deirdre stretched her head wondering what Ben and Woody were up to.

Pressing his nose to the glass, Ben called to Deirdre and waved her over, "Hey, sweetheart, com'ere. You gotta see this."

Crossing her arms tightly across her chest, Deirdre weaved her way sideways through the aisles to the viewing area.

Ben pointed to the newborn chick.

Not knowing what to expect, she slowly lowered her head and peered down at the helpless looking baby bird. Stooping to get a closer look, she placed her finger tips gently on the glass. "Aww." She felt her eyes soften, and her heart melted as she openly stared at the tiny creature. "Omigosh, it's so tiny, so ugly, and ... so cute!"

Chapter 4

A New Family Member

WITH THE SEASONAL wisteria blooms on Ben and Deirdre's deck already a distant memory, the steady *drone* of neighborhood lawn mowers and the sweet smell of freshly cut grass filled the air.

Dressed in soiled work clothes and with beads of sweat running down his face, Ben came into the house after working in the yard. "Phew, it's hot out there. Sweetheart, as soon as I get cleaned up, I gotta run over to Woody's for bird food. That last bag I got for Cody is just about empty."

Typing away on her laptop, Deirdre stopped, swiveled around in her chair, and slapped her hands down on her knees. "Mind if I go with you?"

Heading toward the bathroom, Ben stopped in his tracks and jerked his head back stiffly, "Heck no, c'mon. You sure you wanna go?"

"I need a break from my writing, so I thought maybe I would just ride along."

Ben couldn't help but wonder what was on her unpredictable mind. *It's not like her to be so willing to go along to Woody's.* "Great! As soon as I take a quick shower and change into clean clothes, we'll get going."

* * *

In Woody's parking lot, Deirdre glanced up at a white dove perched once again in the oak tree. *Hmm, I wonder if that's the same dove I saw before?*

The bird seemed to stare back down at Deirdre, his head actually turning as if to follow her all the way along the walkway.

Holding the shop door open, Ben called, "You coming, dear?"

"Uh, yeah, coming." She glanced back at the dove before stumbling into the shop.

* * *

Inside Woody's, Ben headed directly for the food aisle. He turned to say something to Deirdre, but she wasn't there. Looking around, he spotted her heading toward the caged birds in the rear sales area. She seemed to be looking about as if searching for something. *Aha!*

Soon a young male shop attendant, sporting spiked hair and tattoos up and down both arms, shuffled out of the nursery area with a young but fully-grown parrot on his hand.

The mostly green parrot had yellow feathering around his eyes and yellow and red markings on the shoulders of his wings. The striking turquoise-blue color on the parrot's forehead stood out as his most prominent feature.

Looking like a woman on a mission, Deirdre made her way to the rear of the shop. Ben kept an eye on Deirdre as the attendant carried the parrot toward an

33

empty cage in the bird sales display area. *That's it. Of course, she's looking for that little hatchling we saw the last time we were in here.*

The attendant placed the parrot into the empty cage, but he left the cage door open.

After looking around, as if wary about her intentions, Deirdre slowly approached the cage and smiled at the young parrot.

Although walking a little closer, Ben kept his distance so Deirdre didn't know he was observing her and her interaction with the parrot. Folding his arms in front of him, he just stood and watched her closely.

As she briefly glanced in his direction, he couldn't help noticing the sparkle in her eyes that was all too familiar to him. *Deirdre is up to something.*

* * *

Deirdre felt her pulse quicken as she edged closer to the cage. As she leaned over, the little bird emerged from inside the cage, clutched on to the side of his open cage door, and looked up at Deirdre with shining, yellow pinpointing eyes. He then scampered back inside his cage like a bashful child suddenly embarrassed by such a bold action.

Deirdre felt her heart flutter in her chest. *What an adorable little birdie.*

The parrot slowly inched his way to the outside of his cage again. As Deirdre stooped down to get a closer look, the bird stretched his neck out as if to get a closer look at her. Their eyes locked.

"Hi," he said in a high-pitched, child-like voice before darting back into his cage.

Deidre lifted her hand to her mouth and giggled with surprise. The warm fluttery feeling in her chest intensified. Not sure whether to be amused or flattered, she turned to the attendant. "Excuse me. Uh ... how much is this bird? And what kind of bird—"

"That there's a Blue-fronted Amazon parrot. He's a little over three months old now. We just priced the little guy. Twelve hundred."

Deidre's jaw dropped. "Twelve hundred?" She felt like she had just swallowed her Adam's apple. "Dollars?" she asked.

The attendant nodded. "Yup. Twelve hundred dollars. That's the price Sylvia told me to put on this youngster. Most Blue-fronts go for under a thousand, but I guess Sylvia thinks this one's kinda special."

Deidre leaned forward and peeked in at the parrot clinging on to a wooden toy hanging inside the cage.

The parrot looked back at her and appeared to respond to the attention she gave him. Once again, he stepped out and climbed onto the side of the cage door. Several other customers strolled by the parrot's cage, but the parrot seemed to pay no attention to them, keeping his eyes on Deirdre.

"Is it a boy or a girl?"

From behind, a female voice replied, "It's a male." Deirdre snapped around to find Sylvia standing behind her.

"Oh. Excuse me?" Deirdre said.

"The Blue-front. It's a male. A little boy. Cutie, isn't he? I remember you. You're Professor Gardner's wife."

Deirdre nodded and pointed to the bird, "Is that the—"

"Yup, that's the tiny guy you saw in the nursery a few months ago. Grown up now … ready for someone to give him a home. I couldn't help noticing … looks like he's taken a fancy to you."

Deirdre tilted her head to one side and gazed at the parrot again. "Hi, little guy."

The parrot looked back and tilted his head the same way. "Hi," he replied back. He then swiftly turned his head away like a shy teenage boy being asked to dance for the first time by a pretty girl.

Wide-eyed, hand to her lips and feeling embarrassed, Deirdre looked around, smiled widely, pointed to the little parrot, and called out, "Ben!"

Glancing over, Ben replied, "No, don't even think about it. You, of all people, so frightened of big birds. No, I don't think so."

* * *

The following day, Deirdre placed the parrot on a portable perch made of PVC pipe in the dining area. She could tell by the way Ben rolled his eyes that he was still not sure they had made the right decision. Or perhaps he just wasn't too keen about the twelve-hundred-dollar purchase added to his credit card.

Deirdre pulled a small package from a bag. "Cody's perch will come in handy to feed Richard his treats."

"Richard?" Ben asked.

"I didn't want him to have a typical parrot name like Polly, or one of those cutesy pet names like Crackers either. I wanna teach him to talk like a human, so I gave him a human name, one that people won't forget. I'm sure there will be a lot of raised eyebrows and chuckles when I tell them my parrot's name is Richard."

"Richard?" Ben repeated, raising his brows.

"See ... you just raised your eyebrows when you said 'Richard'. I know what you're thinking, but I was just attracted to this little cutie for some reason." Deirdre patted Richard on the head and fed him a treat. "Richard, I'm gonna take care of you. I promise. Mommy's going to feed you now."

Speechless for a minute, Ben puckered his lips, shook his head, and finally found words. "Richard? Mommy? You've got to be kidding. Are you losing your mind, or am I losing mine?"

Chapter 5

Julia

A DEAD RINGER for a gypsy fortune teller and eccentric, to say the least, Julia went about completing her daily chores in typical Julia style wearing a funky, glittery red dress. Her light brown skin and the yellow daffodil adorning her long black hair gave her an exotic appearance emphasizing her cultural diversity.

Julia's bright yellow kitchen, lime green living room, and circus-blue bedroom showed her passion for color. A cross adorned the wall over her bed. No doubt, family meant a lot to Julia. Pictures of her Brazilian relatives hung everywhere including several pictures of her young brother, Miguel.

After cleaning the cat litter box, she flopped down on the sofa and started watching her usual line up of TV game shows. Searching for the remote control, Julia almost tripped over the various cat toys littering the living room floor. Winky, her aging, gray and white shorthair cat, whom she referred to as her baby, reached up to her with his front legs. In the past, he would have leapt up onto the sofa, but age caught up with him. Julia reached down and pulled him up to her side. Purring, he rubbed his head against her chin before sprawling out on her lap.

In response to a knock on the door, Winky slid down to the floor, and Julia got to her feet. The door opened partially, and in peeked Deirdre. Being neighbors and best friends, it wasn't unusual for Deirdre to drop in on Julia frequently. Since moving in next door, she and Deirdre had clicked.

"Julia?"

"Come in, Miss Dee."

As Deirdre stepped inside, Winky greeted her by rubbing up against her leg demanding attention.

"Miss Dee, haven't seen you in days," Julia said. "Missed having tea with you. Me and Winky ... we are watching the TV." Julia's bracelet-sized, gold hoop earrings dangled and jingled like miniature chimes as she picked up Winky and sat back down on the sofa where Deirdre joined her.

"Sorry, been busy working on my book and doing some running around," Deirdre said, looking down at her watch. "In fact, I can't stay long. I have a dentist appointment in a little while." She reached over and scratched Winky behind the ear. "Just wondering, isn't it a lot of work for you to take care of your cat by yourself?"

Julia looked down at Winky and petted him across his back. "At times," she said with a long, low sigh. "When his litter box is a mess. And sometimes I have trouble getting him to swallow his pills. Pets can be a lot of work, but you know how important Winky is to me. He gives me a lot of company."

"Too bad Miguel doesn't move back up here to help you out."

"Oh, my brother would never leave Brazil again. The rainforest is in his blood. That's why he moved back down there. He is still young and working. In fact, he has very important job there. He takes tourists through the jungle and tells them all about the animals and the people and the great rivers." While still petting Winky, she leaned, with blinking eyes, toward Deirdre. "So why you ask about work it takes to take care of Winky?"

Deirdre couldn't hide her excitement any longer. "Guess what ... I bought a pet."

"Yeah?"

"A parrot."

Julia stopped petting Winky. Her mouth fell open, and her eyes widened. "Miss Dee, you buy a *papagaio*? I thought you were afraid of birds. And didn't you tell me there was a papagaio in those dreams you're having?"

With clenched lips, Deirdre looked up at Julia and nodded. "Yeah, I know what you're thinking. I thought about that, too. Could there be some sort of connection?" She peered upward for a moment. "I honestly don't think there is, do you?"

"Just seem very strange you have a papagaio in your dream, then go buy one. No?"

"Yes. No. Oh, I don't know. Maybe it's just a weird coincidence. Anyway, you wouldn't believe how adorable he is. He's just the cutest little guy ... and smart. I want you to meet Richard."

"Richard? Miss Dee, you name him like people?"

"I know, I know. But this parrot has the personality of a human. I was drawn to him for some reason. And it's almost like he picked me out—like he wanted *me* to take him home. There was just something about the way he looked at me and the way he said 'hi' in that cute little high-pitched voice. He truly stole my heart."

"I just can't believe you buy a papagaio. Now you have a little friend like I have my Winky."

As Winky licked his paws, Deirdre looked down at him with a warm smile. "Gosh, I hope he will be okay!"

With an increased awareness of what's to come, Julia gazed down and scratched Winky under his chin. "My baby ... I still remember the day I find him as a tiny kitty rummaging through my garbage bag out front over eighteen years ago. By the way, thank you again, Miss Dee, for going along with me to take him to the vet's office last week."

Deirdre sighed and reached over to pet the elderly cat, who seemed quite content relaxing on Julia's lap. "No need to thank me. You know I'll always help you out whenever I can. I just wish the vet would have had better news for you. How about you? Are you taking your heart meds?"

"Miss Dee, don't worry about me. I'm just getting old, too, like Winky."

They chatted and laughed, and time just slipped by unexpectedly.

Deirdre glanced at her watch and gasped. "Omigosh, it's past three. Where did the time go? I've gotta run or I'll be late for my dentist appointment. As always, it's so good to spend time with you."

She gathered her purse, her shopping bag, gave Winky one last scratch behind his ears, and hugged Julia.

"Thanks again, Miss Dee. God bless you."

* * *

The next morning, Deirdre cleaned Richard's new cage as well as Cody's. Cody didn't seem to mind the new family member next to him. In fact, even though he was Ben's pet, he seemed to enjoy the extra attention that Deirdre now gave him.

After changing the food and water for both birds, she turned to face Richard. "Okay, Richard, time for you to start learning some commands."

"Step up, Richard. Come to Mommy," she coaxed.

He cocked his head to one side and backed away from her outstretched hand as if suspicious of her intentions.

"Come on, baby," Deirdre persisted. "Be a good boy, and Mommy will give you a treat."

Determined to teach Richard to step up onto her hand on command, she bribed him by holding his favorite snack, a nutriberry, in front of him just barely out of his reach. She lifted the treat to her mouth pretending to eat one. "Mmmm. See ... these are so yummy."

Deirdre continued to tease Richard with the goody until finally he acted like he could no longer hold out. He stepped up onto her hand and took the nutriberry in one of his claws. She praised him lavishly as he crunched away even though he littered the floor with seed crumbs.

The phone rang interrupting the training session.

With Richard still on one hand, Deirdre picked up the phone with the other. "Hey, Julia, what's go— What? No. Oh no." Deirdre's eyes welled up and her voice quivered. "Aww, I'm so sorry. He was such a great kitty. I know how much you loved him. Is there anything we can do? Sure, sure, no problem. We'll be right over."

As Ben came around the corner, she slowly hung up the phone and turned to him. "Poor Julia. Winky didn't make it through the night. She wants to bury him in her back yard." Deirdre wrinkled her nose. "Can you do that for her? I feel so sorry for her, so I told her we would come right over and give her a hand."

"Of course." Ben shook his head. "Even though she knew Winky wasn't going to last much longer, I guess it's still a shock when it happens. Too bad ... Julia loved that old cat."

Chapter 6

Getting to Know Each Other

AS THE SUMMER MONTHS passed, Deirdre spent much time teaching Richard to say various words and phrases such as "hello," "bye-bye," "good morning," "gotta go night-night," "give me a kiss," and "I love you." She taught him to sing a verse of "Oh, What a Beautiful Morning" and a verse of "Happy Birthday." She often ran through the house with Richard on her hand making airplane, race car and other sounds.

Reveling in the attention, with eyes pinpointing and tail feathers spreading widely, Richard whistled and yelled, "Yaay."

By his gestures, Deirdre easily learned to tell when Richard was about to poop. He got antsy, squatted somewhat, lifted his tail slightly, and then, "bombs away."

With this knowledge, much to the amazement of those around her, she potty-trained him. Teaching him as if he were a child, she sat with Richard, and when he displayed the tell-tale pre-poop warning signs, she placed him on a perch next to her that had a tray underneath, and said to him, "Richard, go poo poo." Upon completion of his deed, Deirdre clapped and praised him.

It didn't take Richard long to learn to associate the words "Richard go poo poo" with the need to answer nature's call. He frequently ruffled his feathers and whistled following achievement of the task as if thinking what a great job he had done.

Deirdre played with him on the floor and often kissed him on the top of his head. She repeatedly referred to herself as "Mommy" while feeding and having fun with him.

Richard, a remarkable student, learned quickly. He didn't just mimic, as those who know nothing about parrots seem to think. He appeared to understand and comprehend what Deirdre taught him. They completely bonded, the parrot and his "Mommy."

As time went on, Richard appeared larger and more adult-like. The once lean, parakeet-sized little bird grew into a full-sized parrot with smoother and brighter feathering. In particular, his turquoise blue forehead now dazzled brilliantly like a crisp, cloudless morning sky. Even so, to Deirdre, he would always be her "little boy."

On one occasion, while reclining in a chair with Richard on her shoulder, Deirdre read to him from one of her children's books. "And then the birdie says to the squirrel, won't you share one of your acorns with me? Oh, look, Richard, a bird. Isn't she pretty?"

Richard answered, "Pretty, pretty. Gotta go night-night."

"Yes, a very pretty birdie." As darkness fell, Deirdre glanced out the window. *Amazing how Richard associates darkness with knowing it's time to go to sleep.* "And yes, Richard, it *is* night-night time."

After closing the book, she placed Richard into his cage. "Good night, Richard."

Cody squawked, as if to protest.

"Oh, you too, Cody."

On her way to the bedroom, Deirdre stopped for a moment and stared at Timmy's picture on the shelf. *I remember the day Ben brought this cute little lovebird home as an anniversary present for me. I should have paid more attention to Timmy.* After brushing away a single tear rolling down her cheek, she joined Ben who lay in bed reading.

He lowered the open book to his lap. "For someone who doesn't care for large birds, you sure spend a lot of time with Richard," Ben remarked.

"Sweetheart, you're right. I should have paid more attention to little Timmy. He did act like he loved me. But I spent so much time working on that darn book. I'm not going to make that same mistake with Richard."

"That's okay, dear. Timmy knew you loved him. And so far, it's pretty obvious you're paying plenty of attention to Richard."

"Too much time?"

"No, no, of course not. To tell you the truth, I get a real kick out of the way you and that parrot are getting along so well." He closed his book. "So, did he learn anything new this evening?"

"Yup. He learned that sharing is good and that girls are pretty."

"Heck, I coulda told him that." Ben placed his book on the night stand, turned off the light, and stretched out in the bed. "Aah, I'm looking forward to a nice relaxing weekend. Maybe I'll get some work done in the yard tomorrow."

"Come to think of it, I think I'll take a break from writing and maybe give Richard a break from his training. How 'bout I help you out in the yard?"

"That would be nice. Since Richard came into the picture, I'm starting to feel like the other man in your life," Ben said teasingly. He rolled over, spooned with Deirdre, who already started drifting off, and kissed her goodnight on the back of her head.

* * *

As Deirdre slept, sunlight peeked through the window signaling the beginning of a sunny Saturday morning.

From the other side of the house, Richard called out with a loud but child-like voice, "Mommy!"

Deirdre popped one of her eyes wide open, and then the other.

Richard continued calling in his child-like voice. "Mommy!"

She turned and shook Ben. As he grumbled, she whispered, "Ben, did you hear that? Richard cried out Mommy. He called me Mommy."

She jumped out of bed and scurried, wide-eyed, to Richard's cage, scooped him up, and hugged him. "Mommy is here for you, Richard."

"Good morning. I love you."

"I love you, too, sweetie pie."

"Gimmie a kiss."

As Deirdre put her lips to Richard's beak, he made a smacking sound, just like a kiss.

"Wanna sing?"

"Not right now, Richard. You can sing at Penny's birthday party."

* * *

Still in his pajamas as he walked by on his way to the kitchen, Ben glanced over at Deirdre and Richard. With a bemused smile, he listened to the strange conversation going on between a human and a bird. Intrigued by the extraordinary relationship that had grown between them, he shook his head. *Oh, brother.*

On the other hand, he couldn't help grinning and thinking how this little bird added so much joy to her life. She had always been consumed by her writing, but now Richard gave her something else to enjoy.

Ben knew how much Deirdre had wanted to have children. She was crushed when she found out she would never have a child. Now she had something to fill that void, a little pet who loved and adored her and even called her Mommy.

Never guessing that Deirdre and Richard would bond so completely, this new relationship pleased him. Anything that made Deirdre happy, made him happy.

Continuing on to the kitchen, he put a kettle of water on the stove and inserted tea bags into cups. Soon the tea kettle whistled loudly.

Chapter 7

A Close Call

THE DISTANT WAIL of a siren attracted Ben to a front window. Just as he stretched his neck to seek out the source of the sound, an emergency vehicle, lights flashing, sped up the street directly past the front of their house.

"It's an ambulance," Ben said with trepidation in his voice.

The ear-piercing *weeoooeee, weeeoooeee, whoop, whoop, whoop* of the siren prompted Richard to go into a screaming fit. "Aaaahh, Aaaahh."

Deirdre placed Richard into his cage and closed a bag of birdie snacks. "Geez, Richard sure isn't happy about that sound, is he?"

Instead of fading, the sound of the siren broke off abruptly.

Still peering out the window, dread swept across Ben's face. "Omigosh! The ambulance just pulled into Julia's driveway."

Deirdre felt a churning in her stomach. Dropping the bag of snacks, she dashed out to the deck without saying a word. Ben followed, and they jogged over toward Julia's house. Not wanting to interfere, they stood at a distance and peeked into the open front door.

After a while, two paramedics emerged with Julia on a gurney. An oxygen mask covered her face. As the paramedics shuttled Julia into the back of the ambulance, Deirdre yelled, "What happened? Is she okay?"

The technicians, obviously more concerned about speed than responding to onlookers, closed the ambulance doors and sped off with lights flashing and siren wailing.

With his arm around Deirdre, Ben said in a calming tone, "She's alive at least, or else they wouldn't have been in such a hurry."

Deirdre's expression dulled as she stood still with her hand up to her cheek.

"C'mon, Hon … nothing we can do here. They must be taking her to the Regional Medical Center. Let's just head right on over there."

* * *

In the emergency ward of the Regional Medical Center, a doctor and several nurses huddled over Julia as she lay motionless. A heart monitor by her side beeped erratically.

The monitor quickly changed to a steady *eeeee* alarm tone and visually indicated flatline.

The doctor hastily slapped paddle electrodes onto Julia's chest. "Clear," he shouted.

Julia's body heaved, and a defibrillator sequence started to blare, but flatlined again. Julia's body jumped as the doctor applied a second shock to her chest. The heart monitor returned to regular repeated beeps, indicating a steady heartbeat.

Julia let out a faint moan, and her eyes squinted open as if trying to discern where she was.

The doctor wiped his brow.

* * *

After checking in at the hospital, Deirdre and Ben made their way to the waiting room.

Deirdre paced back and forth as Ben sat down and started sorting through magazines on an end table. She sat for a moment bouncing her knee and wringing her hands. Finally picking up a *People* magazine, she paged through it several times before setting her eyes on an article. After reading the same paragraph three times, she tossed the magazine down and focused her eyes on the wall clock. "I wish we knew something. Maybe we should ask somebody."

Ben lowered a magazine to his lap. "I know, it's so nerve racking. I thought her medication had everything under control. I guess nothing is foolproof. Are you hungry? There are snack machines down the hall."

"I can't eat anything right now," Deirdre said, holding a clenched fist to her mouth and squeezing her eyes shut.

"Well, I'm gonna go grab a candy bar."

A few minutes later, Ben returned, chewing and holding a Snickers in his hand. "On my way back, I stopped at the nurse's station and asked about Julia. She told me she didn't know anything, and that I'll have to wait for the doctor."

After waiting over two hours, they both jumped to their feet when the doctor finally walked in. Exhaustion showed clearly on his face as though every ounce of energy had been drained from him. "Mr. and Mrs. Gardner?"

"Yes," Deirdre responded immediately.

He nodded, extended his arm, and shook hands with both of them. "I'm Dr. Lukins, the cardiologist. According to Julia's records, she has no kin in this country, and you have health care power of attorney over her. In fact, she specifically asked if you were here."

Deirdre nodded. "Yes, that's correct. We're her neighbors and closest friends."

"Looks like Julia's going to be okay. She suffered a heart attack. Just as they brought her in, she went into cardiac arrest, but we brought her around."

Deirdre drew in a long breath and blew it out her mouth with a loud, "Ohhh."

Ben hugged her and let out a similar sigh of relief. "Oh, thank God."

"She's resting comfortably, and you can see her now if you wish," the doctor said. "Just follow the signs down that hall to intensive care. I'll be there in a few minutes if you have any questions."

While Ben thanked the doctor, Deirdre rushed into the hall.

A minute later, Deirdre came through the intensive care doorway with Ben following closely behind. Julia lay in the bed with IVs in her arms, but she acted amazingly alert. "Miss Dee—Mr. Ben," she cried out.

Deirdre took Julia's hand. "Oh, Julia, what on earth happened?"

"At home, I feel dizzy and sick. I lay down, but really worry when pain go down my arm, so I pressed button on medical thing hanging on my neck. After that, I no remember anything."

"Wow. Thank God for that medical alert system."

"Amen, so glad you tell me about that button thing, Miss Dee."

"You bet, without that, you might not be here in this hospital right now."

"I don't even remember how I get here. All I know, I see such weird things just before I wake up and see blurry faces of a doctor and all those nurses around me."

"What do you mean?"

"At first, I see a bright funnel of light. Then it got foggy. Then it turned into a meadow of beautiful, colorful flowers, green grass, and trees. I hear dogs barking, cats meowing, and horses ... you know, the sound that horses make. I even hear birds singing and other animal sounds all around me. Then—"

Deirdre's brows drew closer. "Then what?"

"You gonna think I'm loco, but I swear I saw ... oh, never mind. After that, I hear voices and see the medical people around me."

Deirdre patted Julia on the hand. "Now then, you were probably just hallucinating as they were bringing you around. The important thing is that it looks like you're going to be just fine."

Chapter 8

The Mall

DERK, A YOUNG, handsome, and muscular man, stood, with arms folded, inside the main department store of the Pocono Mall. His brownish-black skin, sculpted from the workouts he performed faithfully at Gold's Gym, glistened in the bright lights. Every day, Derk took time from his busy schedule at the Salvation Temple to maintain his physique. He and his girlfriend, Alicia, made the perfect couple.

Nearby, Alicia browsed through a rack of women's clothing. Tall and statuesque with long, dark hair accenting her silken, bronze skin, she often drew appreciative stares from male passers-by. Derk could just imagine the exceptional offspring they would produce.

But even this didn't make him feel better today. Though easy to get along with, there were some things that got under Derk's skin; namely shopping and crowds. This day, the mall advertised big sales, and it was packed with shoppers.

"Alicia, of all days, when this place is so crowded, why do you insist on dragging me in here?"

"I need your opinion, baby," she said, looking at him with her soft, brown doe eyes. "After all, don't you want Reverend James to think the future bride of his security chief is quite a catch?" She pulled a blouse from a rack, searched out a dressing room, and pointed to a bench. "Wait here, baby."

As Derk parked himself on the bench near the dressing room, he sighed and resigned himself to the fact that it was going to be a long afternoon. Feeling woeful like a lost child, he folded his arms across his chest and tried to relax. Before long, he became fidgety and finger-tapped the arm of the bench waiting for Alicia.

In the meantime, Julia and Deirdre entered the same store and browsed among racks of clothing while chatting. They stopped, and Deirdre pulled a blouse from a rack not far from the bench where Derk waited. "This would look great on you, Julia," Deirdre insisted. "You need to buy yourself something. You've been through a lot in the past month. And you sure gave us a scare."

"I feel better now, Miss Dee. I think these American doctors have much power just like Reverend James or the Cinta Larga Indians."

Hearing his boss' name, Derk perked up. He got up from the bench, and pretending to be just another customer walking by, he shuffled through the lady's undergarment area and maneuvered himself into a position where he could listen in on the conversation between the two women.

"What on earth are you talking about, Julia?"

"Reverend James can heal people, ya know."

To avoid being seen by the ladies, Derk stayed behind a rack full of undergarments. As he crept forward, his leg caught the edge of the display, and a pink, lacy bra fell onto the floor next to him. After picking it up, the bra dangled precariously from his hand as he fumbled to return it to the rack.

A prudish-looking, elderly lady with bluish-gray hair shopping nearby stopped and gave Derk a dirty look. Then her mouth curved into a smirk, and she winked at him. "Might I suggest you get the matching panties, sir."

Derk felt a warm rush up his neck and, at first, stared at his feet before looking around, hoping no one would notice his embarrassment. Staring at the bra for a moment, primal lust took hold of him. Before returning it to the rack, he fantasized seeing Alicia in the alluring garment, and a slight tingle raced across his nerve endings. Regaining his composure, he placed it onto the display and turned an ear back to Julia and Deirdre.

Staring at Julia with eyebrows raised, Deirdre asked, "Do you really believe that Reverend James can heal people? For heaven's sake, Julia, I wouldn't give him that much credit." She then leaned closer to Julia. "But what was that you said about some Indians?"

Derk craned his neck and moved even closer to the two women to better hear what Julia had to say.

"There is legend," Julia went on. "Hundreds of years ago, the Cinta Larga Indians in Brazil had a great medicine man who, with help of his papagaio, had the gift of healing. Together, they saved many sick children from death. Family and friends tell me gift of healing remains hidden in a secret garden where medicine man was buried. It is now a mystical land on top of mountain where strange things happen and weird creatures live."

Julia turned her attention back to shopping and held up the busiest, wildest blouse anyone could ever imagine. "What you think about this, Miss Dee?"

"It's you, Julia. Get it. Now what about weird creatures? Weird flying creatures by any chance?"

"I ...well, I don't know really."

The two ladies glanced over in Derk's direction, but he easily blended in with the crowd of shoppers. He quickly turned his head and darted away.

* * *

Deirdre stood by while Julia paid for her blouse. She offered Julia her arm, and the two ladies walked to the front of an elevator and continued chatting.

"Hey, how 'bout some ice cream, Miss Dee?" Julia suggested.

"Geez, I seem to wear everything I eat."

"C'mon, what's one more ice cream cone?"

Deirdre hesitated, then followed Julia into the small elevator. She felt her heart racing as the doors closed and the elevator started to move. *Come on, you can do this. It's only a floor up*, she chided herself. Despite her best efforts, by the time the elevator dinged to let them know they had reached the second level, Deirdre felt queasy and sweaty. As the elevator doors opened, she took a deep breath and rushed out.

Julia, looking concerned, followed. "Oh, Miss Dee, I forget. Are you okay? Why you not remind me we should take stairs?"

"Stairs are something you shouldn't be dealing with right now. Ben and I are quite the pair, aren't we? I'm claustrophobic, and he doesn't like being in water."

"At least both of you have good hearts ... and I mean that in more than one way."

As they sat down on a bench licking ice cream cones, Julia asked, "Still having those dreams, Miss Dee?"

"Sometimes. Speaking of hearts, what about you? Are you getting along okay now?"

"So many things that I cannot do no longer, like cleaning. And I don't have my Winky to keep me company anymore. So, I decide now is the time to go into ... what you call ... a home."

"You mean assisted living?"

"Miss Dee, not to worry. I can still get around okay. And Salvation Senior Living Center isn't far away."

"Salvation Senior Living Center?" Deirdre could no longer contain her feelings. *Someone has to tell her. Someone has to protect her.* "You mean that place run by your church, the Salvation Temple? Oh, please, don't go there. They'll take every penny you have. If you must go to a home, go to Oakwood Acres."

"But Salvation Temple is my church."

"But you know what quite a few people say about that Reverend James. I heard when he was a teen, he was caught breaking into people's homes. Then in jail he finds religion. Huh. And some of the older folks around here still talk about what a con man his dad was."

"But Reverend James is a minister now."

"Oh yeah, he's more of a mystic than a minister. Look, I know I'm not exactly a good churchgoer like you, but if you ask me ... that church and home of his are nothing more than a way for him to steal people's money. He's an egotistical, dangerous individual who's in the business of religion for himself. He doesn't care who he hurts or what he has to do to get money."

Julia hung her head and glanced up at Deirdre as if pondering what she said. "Maybe you are right, Miss Dee. I have heard some people say that Oakwood is better than the Salvation Senior Living Center."

Deirdre hugged her and went on, "Believe me, Julia. I only want what's best for you."

"I know ... I know. I trust you. Maybe I will go to Oakwood."

* * *

When Deirdre got home from the mall, before she even got in the door, she heard Richard shouting, "Mommy's home!"

How did he know? Did he see me coming up the driveway?

She dashed into the house and into the sunroom. Richard clambered wildly around the inside of his cage as if dying to get out.

Looking around, she noticed that both Richard's and Cody's cages were a mess. She hadn't had time to clean them as she normally did each morning. Ben had always cleaned Cody's cage, but ever since Richard was added to the family, Deirdre willingly took over the daily task much of the time.

The moment she opened Richard's cage door, he scurried up her arm to her shoulder and looked her in the eye as if to suggest he wanted to help clean the cages.

Deirdre opened Cody's cage door, and he squawked and scampered up to his cage-top play gym and started banging around his favorite toy, a little bell. He stopped intermittently to chew on the willow branches Ben had put on his cage.

"Whatchadoin?" Richard asked, cocking his head quizzically as Deirdre changed the dirty newspapers on the lower shelf and wiped soiled areas off of the cage bars, perches, and toys. She checked Richard's water because it wasn't unusual for him to dunk everything he ate creating a yucky swill.

"Cleaning up your mess," Deirdre replied, topping off the food dishes with fresh bird food and pellets purchased from Woody's. "It's a good thing Mommy loves you." She provided fresh water and removed a couple of bowls that needed a thorough washing.

After completing the daily cage-cleaning duty, Deirdre turned to Richard still clinging to her shoulder. "There you go, Richard. A nice clean cage … fresh food and water, everything a birdie could want." She placed Richard on a perch inside his cage.

"There you go," Richard responded, selecting a purple pellet and promptly dunking it into his water.

* * *

Several weeks later, a Goodwill truck pulled out of the driveway as Deirdre stood on the small front porch of Julia's tiny Cape Cod house. She entered and scanned the nearly-empty house while Julia completed some last-minute moving preparations.

The mid-August heat and humidity didn't make packing any easier. With sweat running down her face, Julia sagged into a chair.

Deirdre zipped up a nearby suitcase. "That about does it. You okay, Julia?"

"Just tired. My landlord says he will miss me."

"Yeah, I guess this is a bit overwhelming for you. That's okay. You made the right decision. Just enjoy being our guest until you move into Oakwood next week. Our spare bedroom is all ready for you."

Chapter 9

Penny

LABOR DAY ALWAYS meant a fun gathering with Deirdre's sister, brother-in-law, and niece. However, Deirdre worried this day would be more solemn.

While Richard clambered around on his play gym Ben had constructed of PVC pipe, Deirdre typed away on her laptop waiting for her family to arrive. Ben sat nearby reading the newspaper and drinking a cup of hot tea.

A faint grinding sound drew Deirdre's attention to Richard, who seemed to be harmlessly nibbling at the nut and bolt holding his food bowl in place on the play gym. A moment later, the nut fell to the floor with a *clink*. Richard held his head high with a gleam in his eyes as if to make known, "Look what I can do."

"Isn't he smart?" Deirdre said to Ben. "He actually figured out how to unscrew that nut."

"Oh, that trick is sure to come in handy someday. How 'bout he learns to fetch my slippers," Ben said with a hint of sarcasm in his voice.

"Well, I think it's cute."

"Oh, sure. Maybe he'll learn how to screw nuts the other way too. Then he can help me assemble that new bookshelf. Richard, could you please tighten these nuts while I put the rest of my tools away?"

Deirdre rolled her eyes while turning on the radio. She recognized the guitar sound and drum beat of the famous Credence Clearwater Revival song, "Have You Ever Seen the Rain." Ironically, at that moment, rain started to spatter the deck and window.

Richard called out, "Mommy. Mommy."

"Mommy's here, Richard. What's the matter? You afraid of the rain? Do you know what rain is?"

Listening to that old Credence song, she put her hand to her chin, then lowered her hand and snapped her fingers. *Ah ha! Perfect.* She reached for Richard. He stepped up onto her hand, and she rushed outside. Once outside in the downpour, she held Richard out by his legs and started spinning around in a circle. He spread his wings and held on as Deirdre spun him around and around in the driving rain while singing the Credence song. Both acting happy and excited, and both soaking wet, Deirdre pulled Richard to her face and smothered him with kisses.

"Richard, I promise to take care of you forever."

He responded, "I love you, Mommy."

As the rain subsided, a car turned up the driveway, horn blaring.

As the car came to a stop in the driveway, a little girl yelled out the partially-open car window, "Aunt Dee."

"Hey, Penny!" Deirdre shouted.

Barry and Darlene Greenawald

Deirdre's sister, Judy, waved as she climbed out of the car.

Judy's husband, Justin, pulled a wheelchair out of the trunk and helped the thin child into the chair. She held onto her favorite toy, a rag doll with reddish hair.

"Here we go, kitten. Weee," Justin yelled as he ran behind the wheelchair and pushed Penny up to where Deirdre stood.

With open arms, Deirdre leaned over and gave Penny a kiss on her chalky-complexioned cheek.

Judy, better known as Jude by family members, strolled up to Deirdre. They exchanged hugs. "So glad to see you, Sis," Jude said. "Boy, your yard looks great."

"You know Ben ... always doing something out here."

There was no denying Deirdre and Jude were sisters. They looked alike, they talked alike, and all too often, they acted alike.

Penny peered up at Richard. "Aunt Dee, Richard's all wet."

"Richard just learned what rain is, Penny."

"But won't Richard fly away?"

"He knows this is his home. He doesn't wanna leave me. Watch."

Deirdre lifted her arm with Richard attached and looked up. "Richard ... tree."

Richard spread his vibrant green, red, and yellow wings.

"Omigosh," Justin said. "Look at the size of that wingspan."

Richard shook the water off himself and flew up to a branch of a nearby tall tulip poplar tree.

"Oh, no," Penny called out.

"Don't worry, Penny. I've been teaching Richard all kinds of things." Stretching out her arm, Deirdre called out, "Richard, come to Mommy."

Richard obediently glided back to Deirdre's outstretched hand and again shook his feathers.

Penny smiled. "Oh, he's so awesome," she exclaimed, clapping her hands and giggling.

Jude grinned and pressed her palms to her cheeks, and Justin stepped back with a slow, disbelieving shake of the head.

"If I hadn't seen it for myself, I wouldn't believe it," Justin said. "You and that bird are something else. People look at me like I'm crazy when I tell them about you and Richard and all the things he does."

"That's because people don't understand the amazing abilities some parrots have," Deirdre said. "They don't just imitate, they understand many things. Richard is living proof." She wiped water off her face and looked up at the cloudy sky. "C'mon, let's go on inside. It's too wet out here."

Jude and Deirdre led the way as Justin grasped the handles of Penny's wheelchair and pushed it up the ramp leading to the deck.

"There's my favorite girl," Ben said, as he opened the door, reached down, and gave Penny a kiss. "How you feeling?"

"Pretty good, Uncle Ben. Just a little tired sometimes. Did you see Richard? He just flew to a tree and Aunt Dee called him and he came back and landed on her hand. He's so smart."

"Yes, he's an amazing little guy alright."

Ben turned his attention to Justin and Jude. "Yo, Justin, how 'bout a beer? What can I get you, Jude? Just bought a new Pinot Grigio that I think you'll like."

Jude held her hand up. "No, no I'm good right now."

Deirdre and Judy walked to the window by the deck.

"Any change, Jude?" Deirdre asked.

"Nothing good," Judy said with stress in her tone. "Pretty much the same as always. Been to so many doctors. She's had aggressive therapy, but it didn't seem to work. Last doctor told me there are spots in her lungs now. This damn cancer, osteosarcoma they call it, has spread to other parts of her body. When I first heard that word, I couldn't even pronounce it. Now it's part of my everyday vocabulary.

"You can see, Dee, she hardly gets out of that wheelchair anymore. She's in constant pain, but she's so brave." Judy wiped a tear from her eye. "Let's face it, she's never gonna have a chance to live her dreams. She wants to be a doctor. Ironic, huh?"

Deirdre sighed. "Still going to the childhood cancer support group meetings?"

"Yeah, but that doesn't help Penny. She's just getting weaker and weaker. Chemo is so hard on her. Look at her head. Hardly any hair left. Just a few wispy little strands. It was just too much for her frail little body to handle."

Judy reached for another tissue. "And on top of all this, Justin is drinking again. His way of coping, I guess."

"He loves her, too, Jude. He probably feels like he should be doing something more to help. He's her father. He thinks he should be able to fix everything."

"I know ... I know. This whole thing has taken such a toll on both of us."

Judy reached out and held on to her sister. "The doctors tell me its terminal and that there's not much more they can do. They say it's just a matter of months now. Oh, Dee, I can't believe I'm going to lose her. I can see her energy draining every day. I've taken her everywhere. I don't know what else I can do. Whatever happened to the good old days when life was simple and we didn't have to deal with doctors and cancer, and losing a child? Life used to actually be fun. I know it's selfish, but sometimes I feel like I need a break ... anything to lift my spirits."

Deirdre hugged Jude and forced a smile. "Looks like she'll make it to her eighth birthday. Don't lose hope, little sister."

"The treatments aren't helping. I think it'll take a miracle."

Deirdre glanced over at Penny, who rubbed her drooping eyes, appearing sleepy and weak while playing with her rag doll. "She loves that little rag doll, doesn't she?"

"Yup, carries it everywhere. The day she stops playing with that doll—" Judy sniffled and her eyes became glassy.

Deirdre pressed her lips together and gently touched Judy's arm. "That's okay, Jude, don't think about that."

Judy walked over to Penny, picked her up, and laid her on the sofa. "Feeling okay, sweetie?"

Penny nodded.

Judy smiled and dabbed her finger on Penny's nose. "I love you, my little one."

Deirdre gazed out the window and leaned her forehead against the pane. *Yes, it'll take a miracle.*

Chapter 10

Julia's Legends

HEARING THE VOICES out in the living area, Julia came out of the spare bedroom and held her arms out to join the group. "Hey, so nice to see everybody."

Upon seeing Julia, Penny broke into a wide smile, and with a burst of energy, almost lunged out of her wheelchair to Julia's open arms. Her rag doll fell to the floor. "Julia," she cried out.

"Hi there, you little q*uerida*," Julia said. "Oh my, how you've grown since I last see you."

"What's querida?" Penny asked while hugging Julia.

"That means darling," Julia said, as she picked up the rag doll and handed it to Penny. "I call you a little darling because that's what you are."

Penny smiled and giggled.

Julia walked over to the others. "Miss Jude, so nice to see you. Mr. Justin, how is the job at the Post Office?"

"What can I say? Pays for the beer and the bills."

Ben walked in from the kitchen holding two cans of Yingling beer. "Another beer, Justin?"

"Thought you'd never ask."

Julia wandered over to the play gym to say hello to Richard, where he perched, holding a steel nut in his beak. The nut fell to the floor with a *clink*.

"Geeze, I tightened those nuts with a wrench and that bird is still able to unscrew them," Ben said.

After setting snacks, glasses, and a pitcher of iced tea on an end table, Deirdre reached for the nut on the floor, held it up, and twirled it around in her fingers. "Oh, Richard, how on earth did you ever learn to do this?" While handing a glass of tea to Julia, she nodded her head toward Richard. "Who would've thought I would fall so in love with a bird."

As Deirdre poured tea for others, Julia sat by the table and glimpsed up at her. "I wonder, do I do the right thing? I will miss you and Mr. Ben very much."

"Just because we won't be neighbors anymore doesn't mean we won't keep seeing each other."

Penny rolled her wheelchair to the bookshelf, reached for the picture of Timmy, held it in both hands, and stared down at it. "Poor little Timmy. He was a beautiful little lovebird, wasn't he? Why did he die, Aunt Dee?"

"He was old, honey. Maybe he died because I didn't give him the love and attention that he deserved."

"Oh, no, Miss Dee," Julia interrupted. "Fifteen is a long time for a lovebird. He had a happy life with you and Mr. Ben."

Penny sat by the sofa in her wheelchair still clutching Timmy's picture in her hands.

"He was a member of your family, a much-loved pet," Julia said to Deirdre. "So, he is waiting for you, just like my Winky is waiting for me."

Penny jerked her head up and peered at Julia with a raised brow. "Waiting? What do you mean? Waiting where?"

"When I was a little girl like you in my homeland, my mother used to tell me of this wonderful place called the Rainbow Bridge. She would tell me that's where pets that have passed on wait for their owners to join them."

"The Rainbow Bridge? I don't understand."

Reaching for Penny's hand, Julia eased herself down on the sofa next to the little girl's wheelchair. Others took nearby chairs, except Justin, who leaned near a window sipping his beer. Everyone got quiet, eyes on Julia.

After taking a deep breath, she nodded, and began to speak. "Penny, I think pets go to heaven, too. But when a pet like a dog or a cat, or even a little bird, like Timmy, no longer lives on earth, before going to heaven, there's a place where they go to wait for their owners who are still here."

"But why would pets wait for the people who owned them?"

"You see, Penny ... pets ... they no forget the people who take care of them, just like we no forget them. Even though pets die and no longer are with their owners, the owners live on in their hearts. So, the animals wait there because they know the special person will someday join them. They will be together again, and they will cross over into heaven, and they will be one."

Appearing captivated, Penny sat up straighter as Julia continued.

"Oh, Penny, believe me. The place they wait is so beautiful you cannot even imagine. The grass is so green and soft and it feels so good to their feet. The trees ... they have many leafy branches, and they are filled with fruit and nuts. And there are flowers everywhere ... lilacs, roses, daffodils, and fields full of smiling daisies. It is such a wonderful place for our friends to play. They drink from little streams that run with clean, clear water, and there is much food for them to eat. It is very sunny there to brighten their days, but they also have shade trees where they can nap. They are so happy because they feel good again and they are healthy just like when they lived on this earth."

"You mean they don't really die?" Penny asked.

"They die from this earth, querida, but move on to another life, a better life, one that lasts forever and ever. But you know what? Even though the animals have everything they could ever need, there is something missing, and they know it. They can feel it. They are not completely happy or at total peace until—"

"Until their owners join them?" Penny asked.

"You are so smart, my little one. That's right. Even though all the animals there get along and even play together, they have a special feeling when their owners are near. They become so excited, because they can't wait to be with them again. They see their special person and cry out and run to them as fast as they can."

"You mean because the owners ... well—"

"Yes, because we die just like the animals and when it's the owner's turn to leave this life, that person who is so special to that animal who was their pet, will stop for a little while at this beautiful land by the Rainbow Bridge so they can cross over into heaven together."

Justin's attention turned from his beer to Julia. Penny leaned forward appearing eager to hear what came next.

Julia continued, "When you and the pet you loved finally see each other again, you are both so happy. You look into each other's eyes, give each other warm kisses, and cuddle your heads together like you did in times gone by."

A tear dribbled down Judy's face.

Deirdre peered down at Penny and at Timmy's photo in her hands. Penny tilted her head as Julia went on.

"You cry tears of joy to see your much-loved pet. You feel so happy as you and your friend cling to each other. You then cross over the Rainbow Bridge together into heaven. Forever you will be together and no one or nothing will ever tear you apart again."

Silence pervaded through the room. Everyone just stared at Julia with misty eyes, even Justin.

With puffy, wet eyes, Penny glanced at Timmy's picture she still held in her tiny, frail hands. "How beautiful he was," she said. "I love you, Timmy, and I know deep down inside, Aunt Dee really loved you too.

I know you're there just like Julia says. You're at the Rainbow Bridge waiting for Aunt Dee."

For a moment, nobody in the room moved or talked. It was as if time stood still.

* * *

Deirdre and Julia walked to the kitchen. As they stood by a counter bagging snacks, Deirdre threw skeptical glances at Julia.

"Julia, you certainly are a wealth of knowledge about a lot of things that are hard to believe."

"Please, Miss Dee, don't look at me like that. I know you have trouble believing a lot of things I say, and I always thought the Rainbow Bridge was just something made up ... a legend, but—"

Interested, Deirdre stopped bagging snacks and stared at Julia with anticipation.

"Miss Dee, I saw it. When I was in the hospital, I ... for a moment, I think I crossed over to the other side, and—"

Deirdre dropped a bag of snacks and put her hand to her falling jaw as Julia continued to explain her experience in the hospital.

"I could swear I saw Winky in a beautiful place, but then I came back. Miss Dee, you've got to believe me. My family taught me the spirit lives on after death. Maybe, just for a moment, maybe I was at the Rainbow Bridge."

"I think I do believe you, Julia. Maybe you were there. Maybe the spirit does live on for people ... and animals."

Deirdre stared fixedly upward while Julia took a seat. "Speaking of spiritual things, so how was church today?" Deirdre asked.

"Okay, but I don't know. Some people say Reverend James is a phony."

"Huh. I'm not surprised. What has that church done for you other than take your money? You don't really believe Reverend James can heal the sick, do you?"

"But, Miss Dee, medicine men of the Cinta Larga Indians could heal people. Why couldn't Reverend James?"

"There you go again. I thought that was just a legend, just like the Rainbow Bridge is probably a legend."

"Remember I told you about the medicine man who lived among the Cinta Larga Indians hundreds of years ago who could heal sick children?"

"I sure do."

"Miguel told me the story. The medicine man's name was Ubjara, and it is said he could only heal sick children with the help of a bird that had healing powers. I didn't tell you this before, but that bird was a special papagaio. Miguel knows of this because he does not live far from where some Cinta Larga villages still are."

"A special parrot?" With eyes widened and glistening, Deirdre gave Julia a blank stare without saying a word. She then turned her head upward while nibbling on her bottom lip.

"Miss Dee?"

"Oh, sorry. By the way, what's the name of the place where your brother lives?"

"He lives in small town in western Brazil called Aripuana."

"Mmm, tell me, Julia, do you know if logging operations are going on in that area?"

"Oh, yes, I'm sure. Why you ask?"

Dee stared into space as if in a trance.

"Miss Dee, what's the matter? You okay?"

Deirdre then shook her head and snapped out of her daze.

"Julia, what you just said about a parrot reminded me of that dream I've been having over and over. Remember I told you that in this dream, a large, green bird squawks as it flaps past the face of a doctor, and that there appears to be a little girl in a bed behind him?"

"Yes, I think I remember you telling me that."

"In the dream, he also speaks and tells me that there is just one thing that will save her. You mentioned a special parrot that had healing powers. Do you know anything more about the parrot?"

"All I know is, it is said the gift sent by a messenger from God. I don't know how or why certain papagaios get the gift, but the special papagaios haven't been seen in hundreds of years. Maybe caught by poachers, or just died out."

Deirdre sat down and pensively rested her head on her hand.

Julia turned and looked down at her. "Miss Dee?"

"Oh, sorry, Julia. I was just thinking."

Chapter 11

Salvation Temple and Senior Living Center

A SYRINGE PIERCED Florence's arm as she turned in her sleep. She stirred, looked up and smiled. A hand patted her gently on the shoulder.

A calm and gentle voice came out of the darkness. "There, there, Florence, now go to sleep."

Florence, an African American woman in her early eighties, had made this room her home at the Salvation Temple Senior Living Center for the past six months. It wasn't particularly unusual for someone at the Center to check on residents late at night, so Florence thought nothing of it. Perhaps they thought she needed a sedative.

The dim light peeking from the hall faded as the door to her room closed with a gentle *click*. Florence's room, as well as her world, turned dark.

* * *

Two days later, Sheila, the duty nurse at the Senior Living Center, a round-faced, stocky woman in her fifties, wearing a perfectly-pressed white uniform, settled into the nurse's station. A no-nonsense person, she took her nursing duties seriously.

Maria, another employee, greeted her. "How are you this beautiful Sunday morning, Sheila?"

"Oh, okay, I guess, but it's a little too warm for me."

Something bothered Sheila this day. She wasn't her usual, cheerful self.

"I know you're upset," Maria said. "Too bad about Florence. Sorry you had to be the one to find her yesterday. I know how fond you were of that sweet lady."

Taking deep breaths to calm herself, Sheila walked briskly to a medicine cabinet, opened it, squinted, and peered at the medications inside.

In her gruff, Irish accent, she asked, "Uh, Maria, are we administering barbiturates to any of our residents?"

"Not that I know of. Why?"

"Then why do we have these?" she asked, holding up a bottle.

Maria leaned forward, squinted toward the bottle, and flinched her head back slightly. "Good question. I have no idea."

* * *

That same midsummer morning, people filed into a small, white clapboard church. The archway sign read Salvation Temple. A fan in one corner of the church provided little relief from the hot, stuffy air as a few dozen people of all ages and colors, many fanning themselves, assembled in pews.

After checking his perfectly-coiffed raven hair in the mirror, the stone-faced Reverend Jeremy James, better known as JJ, tugged at his collar, brushed the front of his shirt, and strutted from behind a purple velvet curtain onto a stage.

Just as Reverend James appeared, Julia rushed into the church, blessed herself, and jostled into a pew.

His chest out, his chin high, Reverend James made his way to the center of the stage approaching the people with arrogant ease. Though clean shaven and handsome to many of the female parishioners, a small jagged scar on the end of his nose hinted he might have been in a few street fights in his younger years. Pock marks on his cheeks, skillfully hidden with make-up, detracted slightly from the perfect appearance he wanted to present to his followers. But it was his eyes, dark and haunting that froze many in their tracks, seemingly invading their souls and reading their minds.

Swaggering across the stage, he stared out, making eye contact with his flock, before starting to preach.

"My children," he began soothingly. "Matthew, Chapter 4, Verses 23-24, tells us that people with all kinds of illnesses were brought to Jesus from Galilee and he healed them all. Some were blind, some were lepers, some were paralyzed, others were demonized. Jesus never failed to heal anyone who was brought before him. He healed them all."

His voice crescendoed to a deafening intensity. "Just like Jesus, I, and I alone, have that power. I shall be your healer and you shall serve me and serve our Church."

"Hallelujah. Praise the Lord," his church followers cheered as they often did during his sermons. Reverend James believed they loved him and thought of him as the man who could heal them and bring them joy. He reveled in the adoration as they lifted their hearts and minds and checkbooks to him.

"Let us bow our heads in prayer." As Reverend James raised his hands and lowered his head, his mind centered on that little, run-down Community for God Church where long ago his daddy had preached and "healed" many of the hundred or so parishioners. Jeremy learned quickly and adapted easily to his eventual calling.

"Lord, give me the strength to move forward on the path you have laid out for me. Continue to help me comfort those upon their sickbeds and ease their suffering. No healing is too hard for me with your help, Lord. I know many of my flock are hurting. I know many are in pain. Thank you for the power, Lord. Thank you for the energy I need to press forward to mend their bodies and minds. In the name of Jesus. Amen."

Powerful organ music filled the room with an ear-splitting Phantom of the Opera-like effect. The congregation sang "Amazing Grace" holding their hands high and swaying to the music as if mesmerized.

On this Sunday, Reverend James, particularly flamboyant, stomped across the stage with glaring eyes, often pointing a finger at individuals as he went on. "Yes, my children, I am your healer. For no man or woman consumed with wretched sickness can serve his neighbor."

Flames streamed two feet into the air from two large vessels behind him as he continued to preach.

"I shall heal you, make you whole, my children. Believe in *me*. I can help you find health and happiness while you live. I won't let disease strike you down."

"Yeah! Yeah!" Some members of the congregation stood and shouted and clapped their hands.

Without hesitation, people dropped money into offering baskets passed down the pews as Reverend James' emotionally wrought sermon continued.

"Your offerings and possessions ensure my continuing power to help you. Who here needs to be freed of a wretched disease so they can help their neighbors and support the good works of this church?"

An old woman follower, eyes half closed, hobbled forward.

The Reverend stepped off the stage and approached her. "And what infirmity prevents you from being free, free to give to others?"

The old woman answered, "Cancer."

"Cancer?" Reverend James shouted. "Then let us rid your body of the ugly, detestable tumor."

He placed his hand on her forehead, and pushed her back. She trembled, then stood erect.

With a quick flick of the wrist, Joan, the somber, middle-aged Temple Business Manager, sitting nearby with her back to the congregation, sneakily flung a bloody glob to the floor. Although rolling her eyes, she sat stone still in an obvious attempt to go unnoticed.

Reverend James picked up the glob and held it high, blood dripping, for all to see. "Behold, the ugly cancer is gone."

He then pulled out a handkerchief and wiped his brow.

A woman follower in the front row stood, raised her hands high and yelled, "Hallelujah!"

The congregation cheered. Some fell from the pews, mouths wide open, eyelids fluttering, appearing oblivious to those around them. Disheveled, but smiling, they eventually returned to their seats and hugged their neighbors.

Sitting in her pew, Julia raised her brow, but at the same time gave a half smile, and nodded as if to acknowledge Reverend James may have actually performed a miracle.

The sly Reverend preached for another half hour about the need for people to give freely of their personal property for the good of the church.

After the exhaustive service, many came to him and reached out to touch their charismatic preacher. He assumed they believed touching him would somehow miraculously bring comfort to their anguished lives. There was no doubt that Reverend James brought to many what had so long been missing from their lives; a sense of belonging, hope for the future.

Shaking their hands as the parishioners exited the Church, Reverend James couldn't help but smile. *Daddy was right.*

Like his father, all Jeremy James needed to obtain the money and the power and the applause he craved were people, with their hearts and minds set on salvation, looking toward the heavens and openly susceptible to a good con job.

Chapter 12

Trouble Is Brewing

AFTER THE SERVICE, Reverend James shook hands with many of the followers exiting the church. He spotted Michael and Lily, a shy young African-American couple, and approached them. "Lily, I'm so very sorry about your mother's passing at our Senior Living Center. Florence was a darling lady."

As Lily sobbed, Michael took her arm and peered at the Reverend shaking his head in denial. "I didn't think she was that ill. We just visited her a little over a week ago."

"You know these old folks. Suddenly their hearts just give out. If there's anything I can do ... just let me know."

"Reverend, we're sorry about falling behind," Michael said with a nervous quiver in his voice. "We're trying—"

"No need to worry," the Reverend interrupted. He started to walk away, then stopped and turned. "Oh, and take your time coming up with your dear mother's back payments. You need time to grieve."

* * *

Later, Reverend James strutted through the church office door. Derk followed.

Marlena, the Reverend's slender middle-aged wife, long, straight, black hair flowing down the left side of her pale-complexioned face, sat tapping a finger on a desktop. Occasionally, she raised her hand in front of her face seemingly admiring the diamond rings adorning two of her fingers.

Stephen, the Reverend's tall, lanky teenaged son lugged a five-gallon can through the office.

Joan paced like a mother waiting for her teenage daughter to come home from her first date. "JJ, we can't keep going like this. Attendance is down, more dissenters are making trouble, and fewer people are falling for your healing bull."

Reverend James walked in circles, pulled out a handkerchief, and wiped his brow as he often did when under any kind of stress. "Healing bull?" he shouted. "Don't you believe in magic? And can't you get fresher animal innards than that? I told you a few days ago I talked to that old lady and she was going to come forward. I expected you to get a good fresh animal liver or kidney that could pass for a tumor. That goat kidney you got looked and smelled like crap."

What about our Senior Living Center?" Marlena asked. "Florence is the third resident to die this month."

Reverend James put his hands on his head as if having a headache, then pounded his fist on the desk. "So what. They weren't paying anyway."

"So, we can't fill beds, that's what. All the elderly are going to Oakwood."

"Well then, we'll just have to take over Oakwood from that idiot, Wilcox."

Stephen started to walk out of the office with the large can.

"Stephen, a lot of oil," the Reverend demanded. "I want bigger flames on the stage from now on."

Nodding and giving a mock salute, Stephen struggled to carry the can, banging it against the doorframe on the way out.

* * *

Chilly air blew multicolored leaves of brown, orange, yellow, and bright red from the trees, ushering in the autumn season. The sign hanging in the front lawn of the Salvation Temple Senior Living Center screeched as it swayed in the stiff breeze.

Inside, Sheila sat at the office desk on the phone. "Reverend Jeremy James. No? Are you sure? Look again. His name has got to be there."

As the office door creaked open and shut, Sheila spoke hurriedly and softly into the phone receiver. "Um, no, that's okay, thanks." After hanging up, she swiveled around in her chair to find Reverend James, with Derk and Marlena at his side, scanning through a file folder. She feigned an uneasy smile wondering if they heard her on the phone. "Oh, Reverend, I'm worried about the residents. Some aren't looking well."

"Even we have our limitations with these old souls, my dear."

"Of course." Sheila looked down at her watch. "Oh, time for my rounds." She disappeared down the hall.

* * *

As Reverend James browsed through files, Derk tapped him on the shoulder. "What if you really could heal people?"

"That would be nice, wouldn't it, you imbecile."

"Ya know that Brazilian follower, what's her name? Ahh, Julia? When I was at the mall last week, I saw her and overheard her talking to some blonde—I think it was that college teacher's wife, about some gift of healing in Brazil."

"Derk, have you lost your mind?"

Marlena rubbed her fingers across her lips. "JJ, wait. I've heard about that from other followers from South America. That's probably why they believe you can heal. Maybe it's in their culture."

His mind racing through the possibilities, the Reverend glanced back and forth at both of them. "Mmm, okay, see if you can find out more about what those two ladies were talking about. Maybe you're on to something, but I doubt it."

Chapter 13

The Library

DEIRDRE STROLLED THROUGH an aisle at the city library perusing book titles.

A slender woman with gray hair gathered into a granny bun, her white blouse tucked into a black, mid-calf length skirt, and no jewelry, moseyed out from behind the main desk and approached Deirdre in the aisle. "May I help you find something?" she asked, slipping on her glasses hanging from a chain around her neck.

"Uh ... maybe. You work here?"

"Yes. I'm the librarian on duty."

"I'm looking for books that might have historical information about the natives of Brazil, their customs, legends ... that kind of thing."

The librarian squinted, lifted her finger to her chin, and then waved it in front of her. "Aha, follow me."

Arriving at a small corner of the library, she waved her hand across a row of books. "This is all we have. If I can be of any more assistance, let me know."

"Thanks."

The librarian nodded and walked away.

One at a time, Deirdre pulled a few books from the shelf. She glanced at the first few pages of some of them and fanned through others. After selecting a few books, she took them to a table and sat down.

While shuffling books, she glanced across the library and saw what appeared to be a shadowy figure with prying eyes hovering behind a bookshelf, but she thought nothing of it.

The wall clock showed 2:20.

After leafing through a couple of books, Deirdre's eyes lingered on a shabby-looking one with a tattered, stringy spine and dog-eared pages marred by brittle, brown edges. The cover read, *Brazilian Tribal Culture*.

While slowly turning the pages, her eyes widened and focused on the contents. One page revealed stick figure drawings and a high cliff with a waterfall. Another displayed drawings of a green parrot with a turquoise-blue forehead, a white butterfly and an Indian woman holding a child. The text referred to the woman as being of the Cinta Larga people. The upper corner contained a drawing of what looked like a small white dove flying downward from open hands.

As she continued reading, the text referred to a tree with branches fanning out like wings or flames. A drawing accompanying the text showed the tree, but it also showed smaller, odd-looking branches protruding from behind it suggesting the existence of another tree. The drawing also showed an object shaped like an enormous butterfly wing hovering above the tree. She read, moving her lips, following the text with her fingers. *What in the world could all this mean?*

She took time to study a page displaying a crude map of Brazil. A light gray shaded area stood out on one small portion of the map in western Brazil suggesting the region referenced in the text.

With her heart racing, Deirdre quickly opened and leafed through one of the other books and located a map of Brazil showing the name of the states and many of the cities and rivers. Her eyes darted back and forth between the two books. Gazing at the same general area shaded in *Brazilian Tribal Culture*, she moved her lips without actually speaking. *Aripuana. Aripuana River.* Slamming her finger down on the map, she tipped her head back, closed her eyes, and felt her face spread into a grin she could not contain. "Yesss!"

She peered up at the wall clock and saw it was now 4:45. Before closing the old book, she turned back to the first page.

A voice came from behind her. "Mmm, Charles Ryman."

Deirdre spun around to find the librarian leaning forward with narrow reading glasses slipping down to the tip of her nose. "What?"

"The author ... Charles Ryman."

"You heard of him?"

"Uh-uh, not really, but I see the book was published in Great Britain. Sorry for peeking over your shoulder, but I'm always curious about who writes all these books. Just my nature, I guess."

As the librarian walked away, Deirdre closed the books, left the table, and slipped them back onto the shelf.

* * *

A moment later, after Deirdre walked out of sight, a female hand with diamond rings on two fingers reached for the book, *Brazilian Tribal Culture*.

Chapter 14

Oakwood Acres

"CHEAPSKATES," Reverend Jeremy James said, shaking his head in disgust as he sat at a table in the Salvation Temple office pulling money from offering baskets. He jammed money into a safe, slammed the safe door shut, and crammed a wad of bills into his pocket.

Keeping to his usual Sunday night routine after leaving the temple, he walked downtown and slipped through the beaded doorway of a fortune teller parlor. He eased himself down at a table across from Madam Tallulah, an elderly gypsy woman with a rather large hawk-like nose and long straggly black hair.

Her huge hoop earrings dangled annoyingly as she placed tarot cards on a table. "I see wings ... huge white wings above your head ... and fire—"

"Cut the nonsense. Just numbers. Just give me numbers," the Reverend insisted.

She gave him a glassy stare, jotted numbers down on a piece of paper, and slid it across the table. "Okay, but you'll be sorry you didn't listen to what I had to say."

After leaving Madam Tallulah, he approached a news stand.

A skinny old man with droopy eyes, a hanging mouth full of chewing tobacco, and wearing a Yankee baseball cap, reached toward rows of scratch-off lottery tickets. "How many ya want today, Reverend?"

"Fifty bucks' worth. Give me some winners, Irv. Gotta big purchase I hope to make. And play these numbers for this week's Lotto," he said, handing him the paper containing the numbers.

"Here ya go. As lucky as they come. Good luck, Reverend."

* * *

The weeks passed, and colder temperatures brought out the sweaters and jackets. The rustle of dried fall leaves swirled upward like miniature twisters around a sign that read, Oakwood Acres. A carved pumpkin sat on the porch of the immaculately-landscaped, brick assisted living facility.

Inside, Mr. Wilcox tweaked his neatly-trimmed mustache with his fingers and rocked confidently back, with hands behind his head, on his worn, brown leather desk chair. As the long-time owner of Oakwood Acres, Mr. Wilcox took great pride in the success of his senior living facility.

Reverend James sat in front of Mr. Wilcox's executive style mahogany desk. Pulling out a white handkerchief with large, black initials "JJ" distinctly embroidered on the corner, he wiped sweat from his brow.

"I appreciate your offer, Reverend, but I'm not ready to retire yet," Mr. Wilcox said. "And when I do decide to sell I'll probably hold out for a better offer. By the way, that's a very nice embroidered handkerchief you have there."

Reverend James jerked up out of his chair, turned his back on Mr. Wilcox, and grabbed his black hat and coat. After walking away for an instant, he pivoted. "Very well."

Mr. Wilcox escorted Reverend James through the community room where residents, mostly up in age, sat in chairs, on a sofa, and around card tables. The click of checkers, the clack of domino tiles, and the shuffling sound of cards filled the room. The warm flames of a gas fireplace flickered quietly on the far wall.

"The handkerchief was a gift from one of my devout followers," Reverend James said. As he strolled toward the front door, he glanced around the community room. "Looks like a comfy community room. Nice cozy fireplace, too. Gas, huh?"

"Yeah, now that the weather is getting cooler, the residents love it."

"Well, if you change your mind about selling, you know where to find me."

Reverend James put on his hat and coat, started out the door, turned, and looked back into the community room at Mr. Wilcox.

"By the way, you need to be careful. Gas can be quite dangerous, you know."

As Reverend James walked out the door, Mr. Wilcox tilted his head to one side and peered back at the fireplace.

Julia approached from the far side of the room. "Why that was Reverend James. What was he doing here, Mr. Wilcox?"

"Oh, just some business. So, Julia, I trust you are enjoying your new life here?"

"Oh, yes. I love sitting by the fireplace."

Mr. Wilcox chuckled. "As much as you love raiding the kitchen for snacks in the middle of the night?"

Julia placed her hand on her mouth and giggled.

"Don't worry, I don't mind," he said. "By the way, I've been meaning to tell you … your friends who visit you quite often, the Gardners, they're delightful people. The residents sure enjoy that entertaining parrot of theirs."

"Oh, yes, Miss Dee loves bringing Richard here. He's a very smart papagaio, ya know."

Mr. Bowdine, a skinny-legged, balding man in his late seventies, dressed in nothing but white, baggy jockey shorts sat down in a nearby chair, looked at Julia with a wolfish grin, and winked.

"Hi, Julia."

"Hello, Mr. Bowdine."

Mr. Wilcox chimed in, "Mr. Bowdine, it would be nice if you'd at least put on some trousers."

* * *

Reverend James came out the door of Oakwood Acres and passed Deirdre and Ben who approached the front entrance. The Reverend tipped his hat.

As he pulled his handkerchief out of his pocket and dabbed his nose, Deirdre turned and gave him a frosty look. "You're that James fellow."

Ben glared at her. "Dee!"

Reverend James turned. "That would be *Reverend* James, Ma'am."

"Of course, how rude of me. Visiting someone, Reverend? All those who moved here to Oakwood Acres because they got tired of you taking all their money, perhaps?"

"Dee, that's enough," Ben said incredulously. "I apologize, Reverend."

"That's quite alright, Mister, uh ...."

"Gardner."

"Ah, yes, our esteemed environmentalist from the college. Good day, Mr. Gardner." He started to walk away, but stopped and turned. "Excuse me. I mean *Professor* Gardner."

Reverend James' ringing cell phone interrupted the awkward conversation. As he pulled out his phone and headed to his car in the parking lot, he made a mental note of Deirdre's "disrespectful" behavior. *How dare she?*

"Yes, Marlena, that college fellow, Professor Gardner and his wife. Good, good, keep on it."

He tucked away his phone and climbed into his black 1984 Cadillac.

* * *

Inside Oakwood Acres, with Ben at her side, Deirdre entered Julia's modest room and embraced her.

"So, how's it going?" Deirdre said smiling widely.

"Oh, I am so happy here. You were right. This place is wonderful." Stretching her neck, Julia looked around both sides of Deirdre. "Where's Richard? Everybody here loves him, ya know."

"Sorry. I didn't bring him today. Maybe next time."

They headed toward the community room, greeting happy-looking residents, who appeared either old or dealing with disabilities.

"It seems so nice and peaceful here," Ben remarked. "Not much excitement though."

Ben had hardly uttered those words when Mr. Bowdine leaped out of a doorway and dashed stark naked down the hall, butt cheeks glimmering in the sunlight shining through a hall window.

A female attendant, yelling, chased after him.

He halted, and abruptly turned around. There he stood in all his glory.

At first, with mouths falling open, Deirdre, Ben and Julia stared. Deirdre slapped her hands against her cheeks and turned her head to the side. Ben, who started to chuckle, reached out just in time to catch Julia who gasped and nearly fainted.

Raising a brow and winking, Mr. Bowdine said in a calm voice, "Anybody for a game of Chinese marbles?"

The female attendant yanked Mr. Bowdine toward his room.

"Can't a guy have any fun around here?" he said. "And don't make me go to bed. I'm not tired. Leave me alone."

His mumbling continued to resonate through the hall until the attendant closed his door.

Several residents popped their heads out of their doorways.

Two middle-aged residents, Martin and Annie, emerged from their rooms. By their awkward gait and bewildered facial expressions, Deirdre identified them as people with disabilities. Martin held onto Annie's arm.

"Ju-ju-juwia, ah-ah, hare you okay?" Annie said, slurring her speech.

"Yes, I'm ok, Miss Annie. I'll meet you by the fireplace in a little while to play checkers."

"See you la-la-ter," Annie said bobbing her head.

Ben held onto Julia as she took a deep breath and gathered herself.

While fanning Julia's face with her hand, Deirdre did a double take at the two residents. "Julia, they're so young."

"Oh, you mean Martin and Annie? I have no idea what is the whole story. I just know their mama and poppy couldn't take care of them. They get the care they need here."

Ben and Deirdre escorted Julia back to her room. After getting her comfortably placed on her recliner, they turned toward the door.

"See you on Saturday for Penny's birthday party," Deirdre reminded Julia.

"I would not forget. I can't wait to wish my little querida a happy birthday."

Deirdre and Ben rushed down the walkway into the parking lot.

Ben gritted his teeth. "Saturday ought to be interesting ... with Julia, your sister, and Dean Haase, all coming to our house for Penny's birthday party. Can hardly wait for the celebration to begin."

Chapter 15

The Birthday Party

A BIRTHDAY CAKE on the table read, Happy 8th Birthday Penny.

With Deirdre leading like a conductor, Ben, Julia, Judy and Justin joined in gleefully singing happy birthday to Penny.

Henry Haase, the heavy set, round-faced Dean of the Science Department at the University, sat at one end of the table. Although preoccupied with constantly adjusting his toupee, much too dark for a man in his sixties, he sang along.

Next to him sat his wife, Ada, a flamboyant figure to say the least. A gaudy, oversized rhinestone necklace hung down over her matronly chest. Her reddish-dyed hair matched the red lipstick smeared on her lips. Nobody dared to tell her about the lipstick clearly visible on her front teeth as she sang along.

Richard sat on his play gym and joined in the singing as best he could. "Happy biiirr-day toooo you."

Everybody cheered and clapped.

Richard also cheered, "Yaay." He even made a clapping sound with his beak and fluttered his tail. Down feathers scattered and floated to the floor.

"Dean Haase, Ada, it was so nice of you to join us for Penny's party," said Deirdre. "Sorry about those feathers, but Richard is going through a molt right now."

"I'm delighted to meet the darling little niece of our university's best professor," Dean Haase replied. "By the way, that was a wonderful dinner, and now I can't wait to dig into a piece of Penny's cake."

Judy piped up, "Make a wish, Penny."

Penny closed her eyes, took a deep breath, and blew weakly at the candles. The flames waved faintly. Only a couple of the candles blew out.

Judy bit her lip, pressed a fist against her chest, and glanced at Justin.

A couple seconds of silence passed before Deirdre, deeply touched, forced a smile and started to clap. Everyone smiled and joined in.

As the others ate cake, Judy and Deirdre carried dishes to the kitchen.

Judy took a deep breath, exhaled slowly, and peered upward. "I don't know what Penny wished for, but I wished for a miracle."

"If you wished hard enough, maybe it will come true," Deirdre said.

Hearing Penny giggle, Deirdre emerged from the kitchen to find Richard flying recklessly around the house, scattering down feathers everywhere.

Penny laughed and others watched. Richard landed on Dean Haase's head. The Dean's eyes peered upward. Judy's jaw dropped. Penny squeezed her lips tightly together, holding back a chuckle, while Justin and Ben looked on, bug-eyed.

Deirdre cringed while watching Richard's shenanigans. *Omigod. What will happen next?*

Sure enough, Richard took off into the air with Dean Haase's hair piece firmly attached to his claws revealing Dean Haase's shiny bald head. Justin, in the midst of taking a swig of beer, spewed beer from his mouth in a fit of muffled laughter.

Ben and Justin took chase as Richard flew triumphantly around with hair piece in tow like a hawk clutching its prey.

The room erupted in chaos.

Judy yelled, "Get him."

Julia slapped her hands to her cheeks. "*Caramba!* Miss Dee, your papagaio."

Deirdre screamed. Ada grinned and even appeared to snigger. Penny continued to giggle uncontrollably.

Richard landed on various pieces of furniture, but took off again as Ben reached for him.

"Got 'em. No, I don't got 'em," Ben shouted.

A lamp and knickknacks crashed to the floor.

Richard flew over the dining table and dropped the hair piece, with a *plop*, onto the middle of the birthday cake.

He then landed on the top of Ada's head and began to squat. "Richard go poo poo," he proudly proclaimed.

Deirdre started to reach for Richard. "Ohhhh, Richard, no, nooooo."

Everyone froze. A *squeaking* sound broke the silence, followed by a *splat*. Ada's eyeballs sashayed upward. Like pistachio ice cream melting down the side of a cone, Richard's deposit oozed slowly down Ada's forehead.

Richard again took flight.

At first, Penny's eyes widened and her jaw dropped. Then she put her hand over her mouth in what looked like an attempt to swallow her laughter.

Richard finally glided to the floor. One wing twisted outward as he encountered a chair leg.

As Deirdre scurried to pick him up from the floor, her hand brushed aside some loose feathering exposing a patch of skin on the side of his body. A white mark caught her eye. For a moment, her breathing suspended. Squinting to examine it more closely, she saw what looked like the shape of wings attached to a small tubular body. The drawing of the white butterfly she saw in the old book at the library flashed in her head. She sucked in a deep breath. *Oh … my … God! Could this be?* Mental numbness set in as she glanced up at Ben.

"What's the matter?" Ben said. "You look like you've seen a ghost. Is he okay?"

"Oh … ah … yeah, he's fine."

While carrying Richard back to the sunroom, Deirdre stopped at her desk and glanced down at her book manuscripts. She peered upward deep in thought. Seeking to resolve an internal conflict, she darted her eyes back and forth between the manuscripts and

Richard. She placed Richard into his cage and shook a scolding finger at him. "Richard, you bad boy."

Returning to the dining area, she stopped for a moment and stared at Penny, who now sat slumped at the table playing with her doll. The notion of Penny dying brought a lump to her throat. Fleeting thoughts of happier times coursed through her mind. *I gotta do something.*

Soon everybody took seats and calmed down. Deirdre handed Ada a wet cloth. Ada mumbled incoherently as she wiped her forehead.

"Dean Haase, Ada, I don't know what to say," Ben said. "I'm mortified. Please accept our apologies."

Dean Haase glared at Ben. Everybody in the room froze. Beads of sweat formed on Ben's forehead. Then Dean Haase smiled broadly and broke out into laughter. "Why that was the most fun I've had in years. That bird of yours is a hoot. Don't you think, Ada?"

"I must say, he certainly has a unique way of greeting his guests," Ada replied.

The mood in the room transformed into a combination of sighs, smiles and laughter.

"Really?" Ben asked.

"Sure! Don't worry. Lighten up, Ben." The Dean glanced at his watch. "Gosh, I hate to run, but I have a budget meeting I have to prepare for."

Ada, still wiping her forehead, and Dean Haase, with hair piece back on his head, albeit slightly crooked and styled with pink icing drizzle, teetered out the front door.

"Again, I do apologize," Ben said. "Thanks for being so understanding."

Shortly after the Haases left, Deirdre and Judy finished cleaning up the mess.

"Hey, Dee, so how 'bout taking me for a ride in that new convertible of yours," Judy said.

"Hey, great idea."

"Now?" Ben asked. "You're going for a ride now?"

"Sweetheart, look, I'm sorry about what happened. It wasn't my fault, and Richard didn't know better. He just got spooked by something. We got the house cleaned up, and Dean Haase and Ada didn't even act upset. Jude's been wanting to go for a ride in my car and, well, she's here now. Think about this. When was the last time you saw Penny laugh and act so happy?"

"You gotta point there. It sure was nice seeing her laugh and having a good time for a change. Come to think of it, it was nice seeing Dean Haase laugh too. He's always so serious. Go on, take Jude for a ride. I'll make sure Julia gets back to Oakwood safely."

Deirdre smacked a kiss on Ben's cheek, and she and Judy headed out the door.

"Watch your speed, lead foot," Ben yelled as they climbed into the car.

* * *

The sporty red convertible with top down spun out down the driveway. Deirdre and Judy, hair blowing back, couldn't help but laugh at how the much-anticipated birthday party had turned out.

"Do you believe what Richard did?" Deirdre said. "I gotta give him credit. He held onto that toupee a long time before finally dropping it."

"And I never saw anything as funny as that poop rolling down Ada's snobby nose," Judy said. "Like I always say, everybody needs to deal with a little crap in their life now and then. Builds character."

They just couldn't hold back the laughter as they rehashed the evening. The car faded fast into the distance as Judy held her arms high catching the wind.

* * *

Later that evening, on his way to the kitchen for a night-time snack, Ben walked past the sunroom and glanced at Deirdre sitting at her desk. The glow of her laptop screen reflected across her face.

"Working on your book, dear? Ya coming to bed?"

"Uh, yeah. I'll be in soon."

In a little while, Deirdre joined Ben who held a book while propped up in bed. The nightstand lamp glowed.

"Do you really think Dean Haase isn't upset about what Richard did?" Deirdre asked.

"He didn't act like it. And if he is, he's sure to be over it by the time I get back from Brazil."

She nestled up to Ben affectionately. "You mean by the time *we* get back," she whispered.

"We? From New York?"

"No, silly, from Brazil. I'm not gonna let a few alligators and weird flying creatures scare me off. Then when we get back, we can take that nice romantic trip to New York."

Ben's eyes narrowed. "Why the sudden interest in going to Brazil with me? Are you sure about this?"

"You know that book I started writing about Richard? I talked to my publisher about it and he said he'd like to see that too. I need time to finish it. So, he said to get back to him when I'm ready. Therefore—"

"But—"

"No buts about it. We're going."

Smiling, Ben leaned and kissed her. "Okay then, I guess tomorrow we can start talking about what part of Brazil to go to and make the arrangements."

Deirdre gave Ben a sheepish look. "Well, I ... I've been doing quite a bit of research lately, and, well ... I think I have all the information we need to plan a trip to Brazil." *Heh! More information than he thinks.* "In fact, did you think I was really just working on my book a while ago?" *Egads! I can't tell him yet why I really want to go.*

"Wait a minute. You can't have all the information. Remember, there has to be logging and mining operations wherever we go ... and an authority for me to report to ... and we'll need a guide, and—"

Deirdre put her finger to Ben's lips. "Shhh, don't worry. Remember? You already told me all that. Like I said, I have all the information. I even picked out an area in Brazil that has an ecological station."

A slow smile spread across Ben's face. "Why you rascal you. I guess I forgive you and your Richard for embarrassing Dean Haase and me today. After all, Penny sure had a good time, didn't she?"

"Then, that settles it. We'll sit down tomorrow, go over everything together, and make the final arrangements," Deirdre responded, yawning widely. "Right now, I'm so tired I can hardly keep my eyes open."

Ben kissed her on the forehead. "Okay, tomorrow. Good night, dear." After turning out the nightstand light, Ben rolled over and snuggled close to Deirdre.

Chapter 16

Competition Emerges

MARLENA SAT BEHIND a computer monitor at the Salvation Temple office. Derk stood nearby with arms folded.

Reverend James paced. "So, it's true?"

"There's more," Marlena said. "Those friends of Julia's, that college professor and his wife ...." She swiveled the monitor toward the Reverend and raised her brow. "Check out this email from my friend, Renata, at the airport."

Reverend James squinted as he peered at the monitor. "Aripuana, Brazil? They're going to Brazil?" He glanced over at Marlena.

Her eyes widened and she nodded.

The Reverend went on, "They're taking a parrot? So, if what you and Derk tell me is true, apparently they're actually going to search for it ... some sort of healing power in the Amazon rainforest?" He paced, scraping a hand through his hair. "Imagine if I could get my hands on it first."

"Yeah, but you have no idea how to find it," said Derk.

"If there is such a thing, the professor and his wife must know," said Marlena. "Or at least they know something."

The Reverend wiped his brow with his handkerchief. "Then perhaps they could lead me right to it."

Feeling flustered by the less-than-ideal scheme, Marlena rolled her eyes. "Oh, you've got to be kidding."

* * *

A few days later, Marlena marched into the church office. "Here's your damn tickets," she grumbled, practically throwing them at Reverend James. "This flight will get you there a day ahead of the Gardners, who are booked to stay at a hotel called the Pousada de Resto. I can't believe you're really going to chase after them in Brazil. You actually believe they're going to lead you to some sort of secret healing power there?"

"Derk knows what he heard Julia say to that Gardner woman at the mall, and hey, you're the one who came back with all that information from the library! And don't forget now, it was *your* friend, Renata, who found out where in Brazil they're going."

"Sure, but just because they're going on a wild goose chase doesn't mean *you* have to."

"Quite frankly, I don't mind getting away from *you* for a while. Just think of this as a vacation for me and Derk. You just mind the church and make sure things run okay at the Senior Living Center."

"Harrumph, when was the last time you took *me* on a vacation. By the way, I didn't find you a place to stay there. The Pousada de Resto was booked solid. Besides, it probably wouldn't be wise for you to stay at the same place as the Gardners anyway. I'm sure you wouldn't want them to see you there. You're on your own."

The Reverend scowled at her. "How sweet of you, dear."

* * *

Upon arrival at the Aripuana airport in Brazil, Derk hauled their luggage to the curb and flagged down a taxi. Reverend James stood nearby and wiped sweat from his brow.

On the way to town, sitting in the back seat of the cab, Derk whispered to the Reverend, "I wonder if this guy can help us." He leaned toward the front of the cab. "Hey, *sprechen Sie* English?"

The Reverend jabbed Derk in the side with his elbow. "You idiot. This is Brazil, not Germany. Driver, f*ala ingles?*"

"*Falo. Sim,* senhor, ahh, I mean yes, I do. Everybody here speaks *ingles* as much as they speak Portuguese. There are so many *Americano* companies here, no one would ever find work if they no speak *ingles.* But German not so much. Your friend ... he is funny."

"Yeah, he's a riot. Oh, good." He leaned forward. "By the way, do you happen to know where we can find a room in town?"

"Sim, senhor. The Pousada de Resto."

"Any other places besides that?"

"There is a hostel down the street from there."

"Is that it? No other hotels?"

"That is all, senhor."

Derk turned to the Reverend. "I guess that'll have to do."

"Uh, by the way, we'll also need a guide to tour the rainforest. Do you know of any?" Reverend James asked.

"Just go into any of the bars. There's always men there who know the rainforest and look for work."

Before nightfall, the taxi dropped them off in town near the hostel. At first, they just stood in front of the hostel with their luggage and stared, looking like two lost souls. They checked in and settled into their room.

Reverend James wrinkled his nose and surveyed the tiny room, which consisted of nothing more than two cots, a chest of drawers and a small closet. "Not exactly the Waldorf Astoria, is it? A little musty smelling, but at least it looks clean. I can't wait to see what the common bathroom looks like down the hall."

Derk nodded and started to unpack. "Yeah, but if this treasure hunt takes us into the jungle, just think what it will be like sleeping out there. This won't seem so bad then."

"Ya gotta point there. Boy, I'm beat. I'm looking forward to a little shuteye after that long flight, but we have to find ourselves a guide."

"I don't know about you, but I could use a drink right now, and I noticed what looked like a little bar down the street."

Reverend James lay back on one of the cots, stretched his legs out, and yawned. "Great idea. Besides, the cabbie said that's where we should be able to find someone to work as a guide. Come to think of it, it might be a good idea to get more than one of these locals to help us. Ya know, carry our stuff, have a little added protection, whatever. I'll bet there's plenty of guys looking for work. It shouldn't cost much … to hire—"

Reverend James closed his eyes and dropped his jaw. His speech gradually garbled into indistinguishable utterances before evolving into a loud snore.

Derk turned, looked over at the Reverend, shook his head, and chuckled. *Well, I still want that drink.*

Derk stepped outside and meandered down to the nearby bar. He entered the seedy watering hole to find only about half a dozen derelict-looking men smoking lumpy cigarettes and drinking beer. Derk bellied up to the bar and ordered a beer from the bartender whose vocabulary consisted of no more than a couple of grunts.

As Derk popped the top of his beer can, a couple of locals chatting further down the bar drew his attention.

"So, what are you going to do now that the logging company fired you, Luis?" the one man said.

"Maybe I go see if the miners hire me," Luis replied, before stuffing a wad of chewing tobacco into his mouth. "Hey, how 'bout you? What are you doing now? Want to go with me?"

"No, I don't care to work in the jungle like you. I'll stick to driving cab. In fact, I gotta go home before the wife throws me out on the street. I need some sleep. Hope to get some riders at the airport tomorrow morning. Good luck finding work. *Boa noite*, Luis."

Luis waved goodbye, then took a swig of his beer.

Hearing the conversation between the two men, Derk took a couple of deep breaths and sauntered over next to Luis, a short, chunky, unshaven man with a nose that looked as if it went through ten rounds.

Derk extended his hand, hoping for a handshake. "Excuse me, my name is Derk."

Luis chugged down the rest of his beer, gazed up and down at Derk, and made no attempt to either speak or accept the handshake offer.

Derk finished his beer and contemplated whether to try another approach or just walk away. He peered up at the ceiling for a moment and cleared his throat. "I couldn't help overhearing your conversation. If you're looking for work I might be able to help you."

Luis picked up his beer can, and shook it. "My beer is empty." He lifted the empty can to his mouth and spewed out a stream of brown tobacco juice into the can.

Derk waved over the bartender and pointed to the empty beer cans. "Two more, and they're both on me."

"Are you from the mining company?" Luis asked, wiping a dribble of tobacco juice from his lip and chin.

"No, I'm just a tourist. Do you know the rainforest? Me and my boss will be needing a guide."

"A gringo, eh?"

"Uh, yeah. You interested?"

"Where in the rainforest do you want to go?"

"I don't know. And ... actually I guess I'm not really just a tourist. We need to follow some people that might lead us to something we want. In fact, we could also use some muscle, you know, to help carry gear and give us some extra protection. You know anybody else that could use some extra money?"

"Following some people? Looking for treasure?"

"Not exactly." Unsure what to say next, Derk pressed his lips together before speaking. "I think it's just a bird that my boss wants."

"Ahh, poachers, eh?" How much money you pay each day?"

"We're not poachers. It's kinda hard to explain. As far as pay, I'm not sure. I have to check with my boss. How much will you want?"

"Oh, let's say fifty American dollars each day. Yeah, I know someone I can get. That would be fifty dollars for each of us."

"I'll have to talk to my boss. Can we meet tomorrow?"

"Right here ... noon."

"Great." Derk extended his hand. "Shake now?"

The two men shook hands. Derk dropped some money on the bar and left.

* * *

The next day both Derk and Reverend James slept well into the morning. Over a late breakfast at a nearby café, Derk brought Reverend James up to speed about finding two men to help them.

The Reverend set down his coffee cup. "I can't wait to meet this Luis guy. What about the other local?"

"I don't know. Luis just said he knew someone else he could get."

The Reverend looked down at his watch. "Okay, let's go meet these guys. I hope they show up. Don't forget, we've got to keep an eye out for the Gardners. They should be checking in later today at that hotel down the street ... The Pousada de ... whatever-it's called."

* * *

About two hours later, Reverend James, Derk, and Luis walked out of the bar, all of them a little tipsy.

Luis, all smiles, gave Reverend James a big hand shake. "Do not worry, senhor, you can count on my amigo, Filipe. He will come. He will help."

"He better. Don't forget, I'll have a little extra money for you if you help spy on these people I told you about. See you this evening."

119

"Sim, senhor," Luis said as he stumbled away.

Reverend James and Derk headed back to the hostel and plopped down on a couple of wooden chairs on the front porch where they had a view of the Pousada de Resto.

The Reverend scratched his head. "I don't know. I guess he'll do. But I sure hope his friend, Filipe, shows up. I don't want to count on just Luis. In the meantime, we have to watch for the Gardners to arrive, and then we have to keep a close eye on them."

"That's for sure," Derk said. "Because if we lose 'em, it wouldn't do much good to stick around here. I already miss my Alicia, and I'm sure she would be happy to see me come back early."

Chapter 17

Off to Brazil

THE AIRPORT BUZZED with excitement as travelers pulled luggage and rushed around in all directions through the noisy terminal.

Deirdre hurried down the corridor with a pet travel carrier in her hand. Richard's beak stuck out one of the slots. Ben hauled one suitcase, and Justin carried another while Judy pushed Penny along in her wheelchair. Woody and Sylvia, out of breath, slowly caught up to the others.

"Don't worry about Cody, Ben. We'll take good care of him," Woody said.

"Yeah, maybe I'll find him a girlfriend," Sylvia added.

Woody glared at Sylvia. "Don't you dare."

"Miguel knows you are coming," Julia said. "Oh, please be careful."

Ben turned to Deirdre and whispered, "I'm still not sure about using this Miguel character as a guide, and I'm also not sure about this charter flight you came up with. Geez, with all the connections, it'll take forever to get there. And I still don't understand why you insist on taking Richard. Why do we have to drag *him* along?"

"Richard wants to see his homeland, sweetie." She peeked into Richard's pet carrier. "Don't you Richard?"

"For God's sake, don't lose him. He'll never survive in the wild," Woody said.

Deirdre hugged and kissed everyone. She then knelt down and gave Penny an extra big hug. "I love you, little girl."

Penny pouted. "Hurry back, Aunt Dee."

Rising to her feet, Deirdre dabbed her finger on Penny's nose. "I will. See you when we get back."

"Thanks, all of you for coming to see us off," Ben said.

They all waved as Ben and Deirdre rushed to the gate.

From inside his pet carrier, Richard said, "Bye, bye!"

* * *

Hours later, smiling widely, Deirdre pointed out the airplane window to the dazzling rainforest below. Ben's eyes widened as he leaned and looked out at the unspoiled landscape.

The next thing they knew, their small Cessna airplane skidded on the runway of the Aripuana airport in western Brazil.

In town, as their taxi pulled away, Deirdre and Ben, with luggage and Richard in their arms, found themselves standing in the middle of a busy, noisy marketplace where vendors and locals bickered. The thick humid air of the tropics carried with it a rush of sweet, lilac-like fragrances from nearby flower gardens and earthy aromas from fruit and vegetable stands, interrupted by occasional bursts of various food smells.

In front of them, stood a two-story stucco building. Deirdre looked up at the faded red paint lettering, barely readable, above the main entrance. It read Pousada de Resto. "Here we are, sweetie. This is what you've been waiting for."

After checking in, they entered their room and Ben dropped the luggage. "Phew! Could they make that stairway any steeper?"

Deirdre looked around and tried to figure out if she would be able to stay in such a small room. Fortunately, the room had a large window facing the village below.

Deirdre carried Richard to the window and they admired the lush rainforest and distant mountains that poked into the sky.

"Look, Richard, your homeland."

Ben joined them at the window and put his arms around Deirdre.

The marketplace below attracted her attention. "Nice view, anyway," Deirdre said. "Believe it or not, I'm not even tired after that long flight. Shall we mix with the locals?"

"Sure, but I do need to check in with the Rio Flor do Prado Ecological Station."

"I know, but you got plenty of time for that. We just got here. Let's walk around. I wanna see what this town is like."

Ben nodded. "Alrighty then. Let's go."

Deirdre leaned over and peeked into Richard's carrier. "We won't be gone long, sweetie. Bye, bye."

Richard put one claw onto the front door of his carrier. "Bye, bye. Bye, bye, Mommy."

Soon Deirdre and Ben found themselves strolling across the sun-beaten cobblestone square and mingling among the crowd. Deirdre wrinkled her nose as she sauntered by hanging meats of questionable origin. A vendor held up live, squawking chickens by the legs. Other vendors attempted to call attention to their wares, including colorful clothing, jewelry, various crafts, and all kinds of local foods.

"Oh, Ben, isn't this neat?"

"Yeah, I think this is a great start to an exciting trip."

A small jewelry vendor holding up a rawhide necklace caught Deirdre's eye. Wooden trinkets in the shape of butterflies dangled from the necklace.

By holding up fingers, Ben and the vendor vigorously negotiated price. It was hard to tell who won the bargaining session, but soon Ben fastened the necklace around Deirdre's neck.

She gave him a quick kiss on the cheek.

Later that evening back in the hotel room, Richard ate his bird food from a small bowl. Deirdre gazed out the window at the setting sun scattering its remaining beams of light among the tall trees. In the crowded marketplace below, a lively festival got underway.

As she turned, Ben walked up and embraced her. At first, he looked upward as if fishing for the right words. Then he leaned forward. Keeping a neutral facial expression, he asked, "So, tell me, sweetheart. Why did you *really* want to come to Brazil?"

Outside, musicians played, people danced under party lights, and firecrackers popped.

Deirdre fiddled with her new necklace before speaking. Lifting her chin in an attempt to look confident, she finally explained to Ben everything she knew about the gift of healing.

Ben's mouth dropped open as he stared directly at Deirdre. He paced and ran his hands through his hair before reacting. "What? You really believe there is such a thing as some sort of gift of healing? And that you could use it on Penny? Have you lost your mind?"

"You wanna find out more about logging operations here, right? What a great way to tour the rainforest."

"Sure, but I'm not gonna waste my time going on a wild goose chase for some magical healing power. And why bring Richard?"

"There's some sort of connection with a certain family of Amazon parrots carrying the mark of the white butterfly."

"The mark of the what?"

After commanding Richard to step up onto her hand, she lifted his wing and pointed. Ben hesitantly peeked under the wing and gave Deirdre a blank stare.

"You think Richard is a descendant? That mark doesn't prove anything. This is crazy. And what makes you think Julia's brother, Miguel, can lead us to this gift?"

"I'm not saying he can for sure, but he supposedly knows the rainforest. We're meeting him tonight at the cantina a few blocks away. Anyway, it's our first night here. Let's celebrate."

Chapter 18

The Cantina

LIVELY INDIAN AND Portuguese music blared from musicians in the local cantina. Deirdre smiled widely as Ben pulled out a chair for her at a small table.

A large ceiling fan spun over a smoky and festive atmosphere reeking of stale beer. As a young woman with long black hair and wearing an ankle-length, red and white dress with a plunging neckline danced, drunken men clapped, whistled, and howled like wolves.

A glass smashed against a wall. A barmaid appeared undaunted by the shattered glass clinking and jingling across the floor as she poured drinks at nearby tables. Punches and grunts resounded across the room. One man tumbled past the barmaid. The musicians, not missing a beat, picked up their tempo as if suggesting this was standard entertainment for this place.

After being punched, the same man, slender but muscular, unshaven with long black hair braided in dreadlocks, and dressed in grungy khakis, landed face-up on the table smack in front of Deidre. She jerked back and shrieked. The music paused.

"How do you do, senhora?" the man said. He then sprang up from the table, calmly tugged at the base of his shirt and said, "Excuse me." He turned and punched the other man who lunged toward him. They exchanged punches until the other man careened out the cantina door and disappeared into the night. The long-haired man calmly pulled a chair up to Deirdre's table as the music resumed. "Sorry for the rude introduction. Senhora Deirdre and Senhor Ben ... yes?"

Deirdre leaned her head forward and clutched at her chest. "Miguel?"

Miguel nodded, reached for Ben's hand, and gave him a hearty handshake.

"How did you know who we are?" Ben asked.

"I know everyone in this place. And look around ... see any other gringos?"

"You look like you could use a—"

Before Ben could finish, Miguel signaled the barmaid over to the table. "Oh, sim, senhor. You are too kind. *Muito obrigado.*"

"Three beers," Ben said to the barmaid.

Deirdre fidgeted in her chair. "We're so happy to meet you, Miguel. Now I recognize you from Julia's pictures. She told us a lot about you. All good of course. She misses you."

Miguel's brown eyes lit up. "Yes, my big sister is wonderful lady. She take care of me like a mother when I was little boy. Maybe, I should have stayed with her in the States. But I love the rainforest, and I will die here."

Deirdre couldn't sit still. "So, what do you know about this so-called gift of healing?"

"People have tried to find it."

"Oh, I'll bet they have," Ben remarked with an incredulous tone.

The barmaid delivered the beers.

Miguel chugged down half his bottle and looked around before speaking. "Those who have returned say it is just legend. Others say it is real, but is impossible to get to. They say even if you could find it, it is worthless without the link. Some have not come back at all."

Soon, a short, chunky, unshaven man with a raspy voice and a crooked, bulbous nose, walked by the table and stared at Deirdre.

The man stumbled to Deirdre's side. "Hey, blondie, wanna dance?" he said, slurring his words.

She turned away and waved her hand past her nose to ward off the smell of beer and body odor emanating from the drunken character, but he continued to hang around.

"Do not pay attention to this man, senhora," Miguel said. "Luis is an idiot."

Ben asked, "You know that guy?"

"Everybody knows him. He's always here ... a freeloader who is better at drinking than working."

Trying to ignore Luis, Deirdre asked Miguel, "Okay, so what might that link be?" She moved her chair closer. "It's the bird, isn't it? Descendants of the Amazon parrots that lived with the tribal medicine man? Julia told me about it, and I read about it. It's true, isn't it?"

Miguel looked around and leaned forward, eyes squinting. "Even if you could find it, it would do you no good."

"What would you think if I told you that I actually have a parrot that is a descendant?"

Miguel laughed out loud, took a big swig of his beer and slammed the bottle down on the table. "I would say you are loca." Shaking his head, he picked the bottle back up and started chugging the rest of the beer.

Having a firm belief in Richard's origin, Deirdre felt a sense of calm and ease as she leaned forward and stared directly into Miguel's eyes. Without blinking, she deliberately raised her brows and slowly accentuated each word as she spoke. "I have a parrot with the mark of the white butterfly."

With the bottle still at his lips, Miguel jerked his head back and nearly choked on his beer. Speechless for the moment, he set the bottle down and rubbed his hands down his pant legs.

Deirdre leaned back on her chair. "Will you help us? Can you guide us through the rainforest?"

"I will need to see this papagaio of yours."

"Of course. Can we show you tomorrow morning?"

Miguel turned away and scratched his jaw.

After receiving a nod from Deirdre, Ben reached into his pocket, pulled out a hundred-dollar bill, and slapped it on the table. "There's ten more of these where that came from if you'll guide us through the rainforest. Even if we can't find this so-called gift of healing, I need somebody to guide me to where the loggers or miners are working so that I can report on their activity. I'd rather pay *you*, Julia's brother, than some other guy."

"Senhor Ben, I can lead you to where there is logging. As far as the gift of healing ... I don't know. We would need help from the Indians in the rainforest." He reached up and scratched the side of his leathery face. "Also, we would have gear to carry, and it is dangerous in the jungle. I would need help from my partner."

Ben reached in his pocket, pulled out another hundred-dollar bill. "Then, how about ten *more* of these?"

The music got louder. The drunken Luis headed toward a side door and met up with two men.

Deirdre looked up in horror as the men disappeared out the door. To mask her terror, she briefly turned away while Ben continued to converse with Miguel.

"I need to sleep on this," Miguel said. "And you need to show me this papagaio. I'll see you *amanha*."

"You mean tomorrow? Where? What time?" Deirdre asked.

"Across the street from your hotel, around eight. Don't worry, I'll be there."

* * *

Later that evening, Deirdre set Richard onto the back of a chair and fed him a snack. Unable to hold back her anxiety, she rubbed her arms and looked around before turning to Ben. "I know what I saw. That man, what was his name? Luis? He heard us talking. He then walked out with a tall black man and another man that I swear looked like Reverend James."

Ben crossed his hands across his chest. "Oh, c'mon," he said with a disbelieving smirk.

"Don't you see? Reverend James is after the same thing, probably thinking it will make him rich." She glanced over at Richard, who proudly fluttered his tail. "But we have something that he doesn't."

"There's no proof of any of this," Ben said. "You're letting your imagination run away with you."

"Am I?"

Ben took a quick glimpse at Richard, who scratched his head with his claw and even appeared to smirk as he looked directly back at Ben.

"At least Miguel did say that he could lead me to a logging site."

Deirdre swaggered over to the window and gazed out at the rainforest. "And perhaps Miguel can lead us to more than just a logging site."

Chapter 19

Into the Rainforest

AN OLD BEAT UP, green Land Rover, with rusty fenders and hood up, sputtered angrily across the street from the hotel. Although a crisp and warm morning, clouds gathered in the east.

Deirdre and Ben came out of the hotel, spotted Miguel, and approached him as he slammed the hood down with a *bang* and wiped his hands with a dirty rag.

When they got to the Land Rover, Deirdre held Richard's pet carrier up to Miguel's face. "Meet Richard. Richard, this is Miguel. He's a friend."

Miguel stooped and peered into the carrier. Richard stepped to the front of the carrier and said, "Hi."

Miguel shuffled back a step. "Richard, eh. So, this is the papagaio with the mark of the white butterfly? Show me."

Deirdre opened the pet carrier door and reached inside. Richard stepped up onto her hand. She set the carrier on the hood of the Land Rover and set Richard on top of the carrier. With one hand, she pulled up one of his wings. With the other, she pushed aside his feathers revealing the mark on his skin.

Miguel jerked his head forward, then back with an incredulous stare. "*Nossa Senhora Aparecida!*" he uttered, making the sign of the cross. He then raised his arm and pointed. "The region is about twenty kilometers from here."

"The region? Where logging is going on?" Ben asked.

"Logging and mining. Indian territory, too. We leave first thing tomorrow morning as soon as we get our gear packed."

Deirdre squirmed and peered at him with cautious hope. "So, you'll do it?"

Miguel nodded. "Don't worry; I have all supplies we need, even food. Just make sure you have good hiking clothes. Pack light, whatever you can get in backpack. See you in the morning, about six." He then turned his attention back to the engine of his vehicle.

"Six?" Deirdre asked. "Wow. Okay."

"Perfect," Ben said.

They headed back to the hotel.

Nearby, around the corner of a building, Reverend James and Derk lurked just close enough to listen in on the conversation.

"Gather up those two low-life's you hired, and make sure we're ready to leave when they do," Reverend James ordered.

* * *

In the hotel room, Ben gathered some papers and a notebook. "I'm gonna go on over and check in at the Ecological Station. I should be back in a couple of hours. Then we'd better get our stuff ready for this pleasure trip into the rainforest."

"Okay," Deirdre said. "While you're over there, I think I'll just doodle around some of these cute little shops in town. I might have to buy something more rugged to wear tomorrow."

"I have the clothing I need. Didn't you pack good outdoor clothing?"

Deirdre puckered her lips. "Well, mostly," she said with a hesitant nod. "I just wanna look around to see if there's anything else I might need."

Ben forced a half smile. "Yeah, right. Keep in mind, looking good isn't all that important. I suspect this isn't going to be exactly like a family picnic in the park or a girl scout outing. Just make sure you have some good outdoor hiking clothes. Later, sweetheart."

* * *

Early next morning, Miguel revved up the Land Rover. Fortunately, the engine sounded more reliable than the day before. Deirdre and Ben, with new-looking hiking clothes and backpacks, hurried across the street from the hotel. Richard's pet carrier swung from Deirdre's hand.

Miguel gave Ben and Deirdre the once-over. "Looks like you're ready to head out. And you have your Richard I see. Just toss your gear in the back and hop in."

Deirdre, topped with a pink, floppy sun hat, held on to the small pet carrier containing Richard as they jumped into the back seat.

A burly, dark-skinned man sat behind the steering wheel puffing on a smoky cigar.

Miguel hopped in. "Meet my partner and good amigo, Demetrio. He knows the rainforest almost better than me."

Demetrio turned, blew out a puff of smoke, grunted, and nodded to Ben and Deirdre. He then turned to Miguel. "Whaddya mean almost?" He licked his long, bushy, dark mustache. "First we head for camp near river. We take canoe from there."

Deirdre waved cigar smoke out of her face.

The land rover peeled out and jolted down a dirt road leaving a trail of dust and blue smoke.

* * *

Meanwhile, along one side of the hotel, Reverend James, Derk, and Luis, leaned against a rusty, blue pickup truck. Another man, unshaven with a strapping physique, a black mustache and a fiendish guise, strutted to the truck.

"This is my amigo, Filipe, the man I tell you about," Luis said to Reverend James.

Reverend James sized up the muscular Filipe and leaned toward Derk's ear. "You think we can trust these two?" he whispered.

Derk just shrugged his shoulders.

The Reverend handed some money to Luis and Filipe.

Luis shuffled through the money. "A little short, no?"

"You get the rest after we return. Are you in or out? Have any better offers for this kind of money at the moment?"

Luis glanced at Filipe, and they both just nodded.

"Okay then. Let's be on our way. And just remember who's in charge here. You do what I say … no questions."

Reverend James and Derk got into the truck while Filipe and Luis hopped onto the truck bed. With Derk at the wheel, the truck drove off in the same direction as Miguel's Land Rover keeping a safe distance so as not to be seen.

* * *

Deirdre gazed out the window of the Land Rover and watched the town of Aripuana fade into the distance and evolve into grasses, a variety of palm trees, and vines. Earthy, woodsy scents gradually replaced the smells of the town.

The smooth road of the town disintegrated into a bumpy path, barely wide enough for the Land Rover to navigate. Muddy water from potholes splashed angrily about as the Land Rover jumped and heaved up the desolate road.

Sensing Ben's anxiety, Deirdre squeezed his hand. "What's wrong with you? You've been a nervous Gertie ever since we left."

"Demetrio said a canoe. A canoe can tip over easily. If we both happen to lean to one side at the same time, the next thing ... we're in the water. And you know how I feel about water."

Deirdre pressed her lips together and gave Ben a soft tap on the arm.

After what seemed like endless hours on the roadway, the sky darkened, not only because of the approaching evening, but also due to enormous black clouds filling the sky.

Demetrio turned into a riverside encampment as rain started beating down on the truck. The encampment consisted of several wooden shelters scattered among the trees. Each shelter contained cots for sleeping. A small latrine stood at one end of the encampment.

"We rest here and head up the Aripuana River in the morning," Miguel said. "Just pick a cot and make yourself comfortable."

As Deirdre climbed out of the truck, the wind howled. Her hat blew off and disappeared into the trees. She clutched Richard's pet carrier as they ran into a small wooden shelter.

An elderly Indian man, with a face wrinkled like an old catcher's mitt, sat smoking a corncob pipe. Several beat-up looking canoes lay on the ground nearby. They looked like they hadn't been used in years.

Deirdre glanced at Ben, still fidgeting as he picked at one of his fingernails. She then peeped into Richard's carrier. "At least you seem to be enjoying our excursion, Richard. Isn't this exciting?"

Richard whistled loudly and ruffled his feathers.

Fighting the rain, Miguel and Demetrio unloaded gear from the Land Rover. They all settled in for the night.

Deirdre pointed to the latrine and whispered something in Ben's ear.

"Sorry, dear. Yup, that's it. Better take advantage of it while you can."

* * *

After a restless night, Deirdre pulled a tiny bowl and a package of bird snacks out of her backpack, placed Richard onto a wooden railing, and fed him.

Raucous chitter-chatter of jungle birds filled the morning air. Richard seemed to peer upward with alert eyes, and soon, he began to mimic the bird sounds as if trying to respond.

Ben helped load gear onto an old canoe that had dried green paint peeling off the sides.

The early morning sun, already hot, sparkled across the river surface. After they all climbed aboard, Miguel and Demetrio steadily paddled the canoe upstream.

Deirdre marveled at the beauty of the rainforest. Blue and white flowering orchids clung to the branches and limbs of trees like slender ballet dancers in various poses. Birds sang and cackled through the canopy as if to announce the arrival of the intruders. Monkeys jumped from vine to vine among ungurahui and rubber trees. Crocodilian reptiles, mostly caimans, prowled the river's edge, and orange and black snakes slithered across tree limbs. As the river narrowed, overhead tree limbs and hanging vines swayed in the breeze, narrowing the view of the now blue sky.

"Wow," Deirdre said, pointing to plants with flowers in vibrant colors of red, orange, and purple along the shoreline. "Oh look, the leaves ... they look like the beaks of parrots, especially those little red ones."

"You *would* think that, wouldn't you," Ben said with a snorting chuckle. "I believe those are bromeliads. You're right, they do look like parrot beaks."

Deirdre then winced and sniffled.

Ben leaned closer to her. "You okay, dear?"

"Of course, silly. It's just that those tiny bright red flowers reminded me of little Timmy for an instant. He had such a beautiful red beak. I'm okay. This is fun." She sat up straight and smiled.

Without warning, a long, slender, wiggly object dropped down from above onto Deirdre's shoulders and slithered about. She leaped up screaming. "Get it off, get it off."

Ben jerked away at first, but then started laughing. Soon Miguel and Demetrio joined in on the laughter.

Embarrassed, Deirdre threw what turned out to be only a vine off her body.

The canoe glided along the water, scraped on something, and jolted to a stop.

Deirdre's head jerked back. "Oh, my."

Miguel peered over the side of the canoe. "Demetrio, get out and see what we're stuck on."

Demetrio crossed his arms and snorted. "Why don't *you* get out of the canoe?"

Deirdre jumped up and rolled her eyes. "Oh, for heaven's sake." She scrambled over the side of the canoe. Miguel reached out to stop her, but she already stood in waist-deep water.

Miguel and Demetrio glanced at each other, gritted their teeth, and climbed into the river.

After pushing the canoe free from a large, underwater tree limb, they all stared at Ben sitting alone in the canoe.

Ben shrugged his shoulders. "What?" he said, laughing it off with a fake smile.

A school of piranha swam excitedly by their dangling legs as they clambered back into the canoe.

Deirdre peered back down into the water. "Oh, look at all the cute little fishies."

Miguel shook his head. "Senhora, those cute little fishies are piranha. It's a good thing none of us were bleeding. We could have been dinner."

Deirdre's mouth slackened as she quietly sat down in the middle of the canoe. "Why didn't you tell me about those fish before I jumped into the water?"

"Why do you think Demetrio and I were not so willing to go into the river? You jumped in so quickly."

As dusk started casting its shadow on the landscape, Demetrio guided the canoe onto a murky shore. "This is as far as we go on water. Rapids ahead ... can't use canoes. We'll camp for the night and start walking at dawn."

* * *

Farther back, beyond a bend in the river, Reverend James and Derk sat in a canoe while Filipe and Luis paddled.

Derk lowered a pair of binoculars. "They just pulled into shore and it looks like they're unloading gear."

Reverend James put his hand on Filipe's paddle. "Stop. Don't get any closer."

Luis stood up and pointed to the shore. "We can camp over there for the night."

Reverend James stretched his neck to look around the river bend. "Okay, but make sure we don't lose 'em in the morning."

Chapter 20

The Slippery Slope

THE RAINFOREST transformed from active and alluring to calm and creepy as the evening went black. In a small clearing, Ben, Deirdre, Miguel and Demetrio sat around a campfire with sparks flying upward, dissolving into the clear night sky.

Ben chewed on a morsel of dried beef while Deirdre nibbled on a piece of unidentified fish that Demetrio had scooped up from a nearby shallow pool and roasted on sticks over the fire.

Stroking her hair, Deirdre gazed around at the light of the campfire dancing off the glossy fronds of surrounding palm trees. "Boy, what I wouldn't give for a pepperoni pizza right now!"

Demetrio puffed on a cigar, passed a bottle of tequila to Miguel, then picked at his teeth and burped.

Ben cuddled with Deirdre in the cool night air and whispered. "I hope our friends' ability to guide us through the rainforest is better than their manners."

Deirdre giggled and leaned over to Richard, who perched comfortably on her shoulder. "Did you enjoy your dinner, Richard?"

"Mmmm, good," Richard said, as he often did after receiving food from her.

The call of frogs croaking and cheeping and the drone of other unknown creatures filled the forest.

Ben leaned back, folded his hands behind his head, and gazed at the first quarter moon and stars that twinkled like scattered pearls above the treetops. "I love listening to those night creatures."

Just then, Demetrio leaned to one side and let loose with a thunderous, sputtering fart.

Turning to Ben, Deirdre raised an eyebrow and made a choking noise in her throat. "I could do without some of those night creature sounds."

Ben simply smiled.

After a while, Deirdre wrapped her arms around herself to fend off the approaching chilly air.

Putting his arm around Deirdre, Ben gave her a playful nudge "What do you say we hit the sack early, dear."

After glancing at Ben with playful eyes, she placed Richard into his carrier for the night.

As Ben and Deirdre disappeared into their tiny tent, Miguel and Demetrio exchanged knowing looks.

Grinning widely, Demetrio glanced over at Miguel. "Ooh la la."

Their voices vanished into the calls of the night creatures.

* * *

As the morning fog lifted, Ben emerged from the tent yawning and scratching his side. Deirdre followed, now dressed in fresh clothing, a khaki shirt and short cargo pants.

Demetrio stood by a bush peeing and gazed down at Deirdre's legs. "*Bom dia*, senhora."

She turned quickly away and covered her face with her hands. "Oh, sorry." Walking away, she shook her head to fluff out her hair in the temperate morning breeze and sat on a log to put on her boots.

Miguel, stretching in the morning sun, glanced over at her. "Senhora, be sure to check your boots."

"Why?"

She peeked into her boots, squealed, and abruptly dropped them. A brown spider, about two inches in diameter, crawled out of one, and an orange-colored snake, about eighteen inches long, slithered out of the other.

Miguel chuckled. "That's why."

Deirdre watched as the spider and snake slowly made their way into the underbrush. "Aww, look at that cute little spider. And the snake is so beautiful. They just wanted a nice place to sleep, that's all."

Miguel shook his head from side to side. "Uhh, yeah, if you say so, senhora."

Fidgeting with her hair, Deirdre crossed and uncrossed her legs while scoping out the surrounding area.

"Ben, I have to ... you know."

"Well, look around. There's plenty of places to go."

She glared at him and stomped off into the bushes. After a while, she emerged, swatting insects.

Miguel and Demetrio packed up the tents and gathered gear. "We go now," Miguel commanded.

They set out into the forest with Miguel and Demetrio leading the way, slicing through dense vegetation. A chorus of creature sounds rang through the trees. Ben gazed and took pictures. Deirdre continued to swat away at insects. Richard held onto the side of his carrier with one claw. The group stopped on a cliff overlooking the rushing Aripuana River about forty or fifty feet below.

Ben stepped to the edge, set his backpack on the ground, drew in a deep breath, and took out his camera. "Are those the rapids you mentioned, Miguel?"

"Yes, senhor. So beautiful, but can be dangerous."

"Looks like something out of one of my environmental magazines ... so undisturbed, so pristine," Ben said, edging closer and closer, clicking shot after shot.

"Senhor Ben, if I were you I would not get so close to—"

Just then, the loose earth beneath Ben gave way. He dropped his camera and started to tumble down the steep embankment, but grabbed and held on to a thick, exposed shrub root.

Miguel reached out to him, and just as he was about to grasp Ben's hand, the root pulled partially out of the ground putting Ben out of reach.

Ben's arm and hand trembled as his strength waned. His fingers unraveled from the root, and he found himself sliding down the steep, muddy embankment. Miguel's distraught-filled face and outstretched arm faded away from Ben's view. "Eeeeooooowww," he yelled as he zoomed through the mud and bounced on his butt down the murky cliff face. He splashed into the rushing water below, tumbled over a small waterfall, temporarily vanished under the water, and popped up in a calm pool downstream.

Deirdre doubled over and screamed. "Oh, no! Help, help! Ben, Ben." Her calls echoed throughout the valley.

While he clung onto the side of a large rock in the pool below the waterfall, the others dashed down the hill at a manic pace.

Demetrio pointed at the water's edge and yelled, "*Jacare!*"

"What's Jacare?" Deirdre shouted while running in circles.

"Caimans ... you know ... crocodiles," Miguel responded.

"What? Where?" Deirdre shouted with a harried, wild look on her face, pulling at her hair.

Caimans turned, splashed, and converged on Ben who waved his arm at the others. "I'm okay," he shouted. "Dee, I'm okay."

"Senhor Ben, quickly, get onto the rock," Miguel hollered.

147

Disoriented and gasping for breath, Ben splashed wildly in the water, but then stopped and looked up. In front of him, he saw the image of his mother kneeling, stretching her arm out to him with a frantic look on her face. He heard her voice calling, *Benjamin, Benjamin, grab my hand.* For an instant he hesitated, then reached for her.

Shaking his head, he realized he had grabbed hold of the rock, not her hand, and he clawed his way out of the water. The caimans closed in, and he pulled himself up onto the rock just as one cruised by his feet.

Deirdre paced and bit at her nails.

Demetrio pointed to a large overhanging vine above the rock. "Senhor Ben, reach for the vine."

Ben looked up, squinted to get the water out of his eyes, and jumped, but missed his target. He jumped again, grabbed the vine, but his hand slipped off, and one leg splashed into the water. A caiman whirled.

Deirdre screamed.

Miguel watched as Ben stood up, leaped, and grabbed the vine.

"Swing yourself to shore, Senhor Ben."

"I can't."

A caiman, with mouth wide open, emerged from behind the rock. Ben, clutching the vine, heart racing, leaped and swung himself toward shore. Barely missing a tree trunk in his path, he landed on the riverbank with legs dangling in the water. As a caiman approached, he kicked his legs wildly and scrambled up the bank to safety.

Deirdre let out a huge breath, rushed over and threw her arms around him. "Way to go, Indiana Jones. Don't you ever do something that stupid again."

Soaking wet, Ben struggled to catch his breath. "Water—I hate water."

Deirdre broke into a smile and shaky laughter. "What took you so long to grab hold of that rock anyway?"

Ben inhaled and exhaled deeply. "You're going to think this is weird, but when I was in that water, I sort of had a flashback to the time when I was a little boy and almost drowned in my parents' pool. My mother saved me then, and ... all I can tell you is ... she saved me again."

"Oh, I know that left a mark on you forever. Thank God you're alright."

"I thought you didn't believe in God."

"I never said that, silly. Of course, I believe in God. I just find it hard to believe that there is a life after death, that's all. And right now, I'm glad *you* didn't have to find out."

Chapter 21

The Loggers

SLASHING THROUGH THE vine-laced underbrush, Ben walked at Miguel's side as the weary group continued on for hours without incident. Soon, a distant *whirring* sound resonated through the forest, becoming louder as they neared the edge of the canopy.

Although still recovering from his exhausting ordeal at the river, Ben picked up his pace in anticipation of what lay ahead. Not the case for Deirdre, who fell behind, legs wobbling with each step. Ben ran back to her and took Richard's carrier from her drooping arms. "Here, sit and take a rest," he said, pointing to a tree stump.

The sinking afternoon sun allowed a welcome cool breeze to pass through the usual muggy jungle air.

Deirdre lifted her head and wrinkled her nose. "What's that smell? Reminds me of when you're mowing the lawn at home. And what's that awful noise?"

"That, my dear, is gasoline and chain saws ... the main reason I came here. Remember?"

"Loggers up ahead," said Miguel.

Ben helped Deirdre to her feet and turned toward the direction of the noise. "Ah ha, I can't wait to see this."

They emerged from the wooded area and stopped at the edge of a clearing that spanned a hundred yards or so. The hot sun burst upon them as if stepping into an oven. Along one side of the clearing, chain saws blared, sawdust and blue smoke filled the air, and tall trees crashed and thumped to the ground. Trucks loaded with logs and noisy earth-moving vehicles drove about.

Ben surveyed the scene and shook his head in disgust. "How long will it be before the entire rainforest is destroyed and the wildlife gone in the name of progress?"

As Deirdre stepped into the clearing waving dust away from her face, a few cat-call whistles, *ah carambas* and an *olá bébé* resounded from men in the field. Miguel and Demetrio turned to each other and chatted quietly.

A man wearing a white hard hat and holding a clipboard stood about twenty yards away in the clearing barking orders at laborers.

"That's got to be a foreman or supervisor of some sort. I'd sure like to talk to him," Ben said in a stern voice.

Demetrio tapped Ben on the shoulder. "Pete."

"Huh?"

"Pete. His name is Pete."

"You know him?"

Leaning back against a tree, Miguel interrupted, "Yeah, we know 'em. Our paths have crossed a few times. I guess he's okay ... as okay as a logger can be.

He has to do what they tell 'em to do. I know he gives much work for some of the men in town. But I do not like what they are doing to the rainforest."

Ben started to stomp out into the clearing. Deirdre stretched her arm out toward him. "Ben ... now be nice."

As Ben approached, Pete turned toward him wiping sweat from his neck with a small towel. With a skeptical leer on his face, he glanced over at the forlorn travelers at the edge of the clearing and walked up to Ben. He extended his hand. "Professor Gardner by any chance?"

"Geez, does everybody know everybody around here?" Ben said, shaking Pete's hand.

"Yup! And I know about the commission made up mostly of environmentalists investigating the impact of what we're doing here. Your name came up as one of the key investigators. I know what you're thinking. How did I know you were him? Well, mostly just a good guess, but look at you. You don't look like a local looking for a job. You have college professor written all over you."

Ben chuckled. "I guess you're right. Now that I'm here, I sure have a lot of questions, but actually, my wife, standing over there—"

Pete lifted his gaze toward the edge of the clearing. "With Miguel and Demetrio?"

"Yeah, my wife, along with her pet parrot, is actually here for another reason, but don't ask. Anyway, before moving on, I'd sure appreciate some of your time."

"Sure, no problem."

Together, Ben and Pete strolled over to where Deirdre and Miguel stood chatting. Demetrio sat on the ground, chewed on a blade of grass, and rolled his eyes as they approached.

Pete gave Miguel and Demetrio a cautious smile as he folded his arms in a defensive manner. "Well, well, gentlemen, good to see you again."

Demetrio lit a cigar, shook out the match, rose to his feet, and nodded.

Miguel grimaced. "Hi, Pete, looks like you're making sure we will have *no* trees left in the rainforest. Your company will be very proud of you."

"We're doing what we have to do, Miguel. I'm not here to make a moral judgment about what's right and what's wrong. Okay? I'm just doin' my job."

In an attempt to change the conversation, Ben put his arm around Deirdre. "Um, this is my wife, Deirdre."

"How do you do? This is hardly a place for a pretty lady like you." With a raised brow, he peeked down at the pet carrier, but said nothing more.

Pete glimpsed up at the darkening sky. "Look, we're about to call it a day, and I'm sure you folks are ready to put your feet up. Why don't you camp here for the night? I suppose the good professor wants to interview me."

Pete then faced Miguel. "And Miguel, I'm sure we can put our differences aside this evening for the sake of these good folks. You still playing for the Aripuana soccer team? I heard they're doing pretty good this year."

"Yeah, I'm still kick'n that ball around. We have a good season going."

"You'll have to bring me up to speed. I'd like to get in to see one of those games sometime."

Pete pointed to a man leaning over a fire pit with blue smoke whirling all around him. "Our cook, Antonio, makes a mean roasted wild boar, and his frog legs are to die for. He's already got them going over there."

"Staying the night sounds like a good idea," Deirdre said. She then raised her upper lip and shrugged half-heartedly. "But I'm not really very hungry ... honest."

Ben's stomach rumbled. "Well, I am."

Demetrio licked his lips. "*Javali* ... sounds great."

"Yes, it has been a long day," Miguel said.

Ben put his hands out with palms up. "Then it looks like we're spending the night."

Pete pointed over to a grassy area. "Some of the men bed down in the trucks, but most of us just sleep under the stars. Make yourselves comfortable."

Dozens of grubby-looking men with dirt-spattered shirts, jeans, and faces gathered around the fire pit and a table containing various condiments. Soon the clink and clatter of tin plates echoed across the worksite as they sat on the grass, duffle bags and logs gobbling down frog legs and sopping up greasy roast pig. Some drank from jugs of water; others guzzled down beer from brown bottles.

Showing more refined table manners, Ben ate along with the others.

Deirdre sat on a tree stump and squirmed. She searched in her backpack for food, but seemed uninterested in the same old stuff they had been eating for the last couple of days. She peered over at Ben who talked with Antonio.

After a few minutes, Antonio walked over to Deirdre with a plate of baked sweet potato, cut up mango, guava, banana, and some other unidentifiable fruit. He handed it to her without saying a word, nodded making only brief eye contact, and drew back.

Deirdre smiled. "Oh, thank you."

He bowed while backing away. "*De nada*, senhora."

She brought her hand to her lips and threw Ben a kiss across the field.

Ben finished eating, wandered over, and sat by her as she munched on the fruit.

She prepared a small leaf full of cut-up fruit and fed it to Richard inside his pet carrier.

"Mmmm good," Richard said.

After about an hour, the clanking of tin plates and jibber jabber among the workers quieted, and most everybody bedded down for the night.

Ben and Pete sat on tiny folding stools by Pete's two-foot square wooden table he referred to as his field office. A propane lantern burned brightly on the table as the two men talked for hours. Ben scribbled notes as Pete responded to his questions.

Ben looked at his watch and noticed it was nearly three o'clock in the morning. He shook Pete's hand, put his notepad away, and joined Deirdre, fast asleep on the grass with her arms around Richard's pet carrier.

At daybreak, Ben's eyes peeled open to the sound of voices and the rustle of men milling around. He sat up to find Deirdre, Miguel and Demetrio packing up and ready to leave. Ben rubbed his eyes, grabbed a nearby bottle half-full of water and splashed the water across his face.

Pete strolled up to Ben. "Looks like your gang is ready to head out. Antonio packed up some more food for you guys. Miguel and your wife already put it into your knapsacks."

Ben extended his arm to Pete and they shook hands. "Can't thank you enough for your time and hospitality, Pete."

"No problem. Be careful on the rest of your journey."

Ben joined the others.

"Well, sleepyhead, did Pete give you any worthwhile information last night?" Deirdre asked.

"He sure did, and more. We got off on a bit of a tangent. He told me stories about the fighting that used to go on here years ago among the loggers, miners, rubber prospectors and the local Indians."

"Really? Fighting? Here?"

"Apparently a lot of men actually lost their lives, both the Indians and the so-called white invaders."

"Okay, but the loggers and the Indians are still here. Right? What if they start fighting again while *we're* here?"

"I don't think you have to worry. Pete said there's been some sort of informal agreement for the loggers and miners to stay on this side of a small stream just south of here." Ben pointed. "It's over that way."

Deirdre glanced over at the loggers. "Sure looks like they're cutting down trees over there to me! Are you sure the workers know that?"

"When I asked Pete just how much land they planned to clear he said they'll clear up to that small stream and no further for now. They wanna leave the Indians alone on the other side."

"That sounds like a good idea to me."

"But his company is talking about the possibility of continuing on the far side of the stream. Pete also said a mining company is already planning to cut a road to the other side to prospect for diamonds over there."

Miguel turned and faced Ben. "That would be bad. Indians who have little contact outside their villages live on the other side of the stream. That could cause the fighting to start all over again."

Deirdre pressed her lips together, swallowed hard, and motioned. "We're not going that way, right?"

Miguel smirked and started walking in that direction. "We're not loggers or miners, but if you want to find what you came here for, we've got to go that way."

Ben shrugged his shoulders. "I guess we're going that way."

As Ben and Demetrio followed Miguel past the forest workers, Deirdre stood firm and crossed her arms. Ben stopped and looked back.

A couple of loggers moved close and gawked at Deirdre with smiles that slowly widened. It was obvious they hadn't seen a woman in quite a while. A flush swept across her face. She dashed off, accelerated into a sprint, and joined Ben. They hiked into the canopy and caught up to Miguel and Demetrio.

"Hold on, Miguel," Ben yelled. "Are you sure about this? Going into Indian country?"

"Trust me, senhor."

Chapter 22

The Village

THE PIERCING SHRIEK of tree frogs, the call of birds and other creatures, and the faint odor of swampy methane filled the rainforest air. After trudging out of a cluster of trees and tangled underbrush, the group found themselves standing before acres of colorful water lilies.

Deirdre sucked in a quick breath and stared out into the sea of white and pink flowers. She reached out to touch one.

Demetrio grabbed her shirttail. "Careful, senhora. The water and mud underneath could be deep."

"But I hardly see any water."

"The lilies ... they live on *matupas.*"

"Mat whats?"

"Ah yes, "Matupas ... floating mats of vegetation that grow on flooded grasslands," Ben explained. "Right, Demetrio?"

"Sim, Senhor Ben."

Deirdre shook her head from side to side unable to take her eyes off the unusual landscape. "Beautiful, just breathtaking."

From within his pet carrier, Richard chimed in, "Pretty, pretty."

They all chuckled.

"We must go this way," Demetrio said, pointing to the one side.

Even after getting around the flooded area with the floating islands of lilies and other plant life, it wasn't long before they found themselves slogging through a swamp.

Ankle deep in mud, Deirdre frowned and complained as she struggled through the muck. Every time she pulled her leg out of the mud, the swamp made a gushy, sucking sound as if trying to swallow her. Wafts of swamp gases made her nose tingle. She held Richard's pet carrier on her shoulder with one hand while holding on to Ben's arm with the other.

Richard whimpered, apparently expressing his own dislike of the odors.

The swamp evolved into a small stream. Wading through the knee-deep water, they held their gear high until a small path appeared.

"You okay, dear?" Deirdre asked Ben.

Ben nodded. "This is nothing compared to the water I was in earlier."

They trudged out of the water and stopped to rest.

Miguel slid his backpack off his shoulder and set it on the ground. "Welcome to Indian territory, senhora. That was the small stream Pete told us about."

After calmly lighting up a cigar, Demetrio looked back at Deirdre. "Are you willing to give blood?"

Deirdre flinched her head back slightly and glared at Demetrio. "Am I willing to give blood? What on earth are you talking about?"

"Just wondering. If you are, then you won't mind if that little bloodsucker stays on you," he said, pointing to a small, black, slimy leech firmly attached to her calf.

She looked down, threw her hands in the air and danced around like doing the Irish Jig. "Get it off," she yelled. "Get it off."

Demetrio casually walked up to her, took a puff of his cigar, bent down, and without saying a word, thrust the lit end of the cigar onto the leech. It wiggled and fell to the ground.

She inspected her leg to see, to her relief, the leech was gone, and her leg had hardly a mark on it.

"Thanks, I think," she said with hesitation in her voice. "Are there any more?"

"No, senhora, none that I can see."

The group proceeded along the path. Then, as if all the creatures of the forest had been turned off with a switch, the usually noisy rainforest became eerily quiet.

Miguel stopped, put his arm up in front of the others and looked around. "Shh ... listen."

Ben halted behind Miguel's outstretched arm. "I don't hear anything."

"That's what I mean. The animals are quiet. We're not alone. We're being watched."

While gazing around, Deirdre stumbled over a fallen tree limb. "Oooh," she cried out, and found herself rolling on the ground. Richard's carrier rolled next to her. As she lifted her head, a human skull popped up from the soft mud, like a Jack-in-the-box, just inches from her face. The hollow eye sockets of the skull seemed to stare directly into her eyes. The sound of her heartbeat thrashed in her ears. She jerked back and let out a primal scream.

The others scrambled back to her.

From inside his carrier, Richard said, "Pretty, pretty."

She reached for Richard's carrier as Ben helped her to her feet.

An arrow protruded ominously up from the body of the skeleton beneath the skull.

"Must be somebody pissed off the Indians," Demetrio said while re-lighting his cigar.

"Are these Indians still dangerous?" Ben asked.

"Why don't you ask him?" Demetrio replied, pointing down at the skeleton.

Miguel chimed in, "We must be getting close to a village. They don't see many white men. Just stay with me and do as I say if you want their help. We should be okay as long as we show we don't mean them any harm."

"If we see any, okay if I take pictures of them?" Ben asked while pulling out his camera.

Miguel simply glared at him.

Ben fumbled to tuck his camera back into his backpack.

The group crossed an open field of scrub grasses and crops of some kind. Ahead, mountains shrouded by clouds rose above the horizon. The clearing gave way to a cluster of small trees.

Deirdre yawned and leaned against a tree trunk. "Can we rest?"

They all stopped. Deirdre held Richard's carrier close to her face and peeked in at him.

"Are you okay, my little Richard?"

"Yeah," he responded. Then after a moment of silence, he announced, "Pretty, pretty."

"Now what do you see that is so pretty, Richard?"

An uneasy silence overcame the immediate vicinity.

Deirdre slowly lowered Richard's pet carrier only to find the bronze face of a steely-eyed native with black hair in a bowl-shaped haircut standing within inches of her nose. He stared, stone-faced, then grinned widely, white teeth seemingly too large for his mouth, and one front tooth conspicuously missing.

Deirdre gulped, cleared her throat, and gasped in a voice that came out in a squeaky high pitch. "Ben?"

Holding her head perfectly still, she darted her eyes back and forth, scanning the area, only to find several other Indians pointing spears and bows and arrows at the others. Their scanty clothes and faces with red painted markings reminded her of pictures she had seen in *National Geographic*. Her heart jumped into her throat.

* * *

Soon the four travelers found themselves prodded into a clearing surrounded by huts made of tree limbs and grass. Dead monkeys hung from poles. Children, nearly naked except for loin cloths, ran about chatting and laughing.

An older white man with a balding head, a long grey beard, and dressed in faded khakis, sat on a crude wooden stool peering into a youngster's ear. He appeared strangely out of place among all the dark-skinned natives in the village. A tall middle-aged Indian with black hair in a bowl haircut, adorned with brightly colored animal skins, jewelry, and macaw feathers, stood next to him with a deadpan expression, arms folded.

Without looking up at them, the white man spoke calmly in a strong British accent. "What is your business here, mates?"

The four of them glanced awkwardly at each other.

Miguel finally spoke up. "My name is Miguel from Aripuana, and this is my partner Demetrio, and—"

Ben stepped forward. "I'm Professor Ben Gardner. This is my wife, Deirdre. I teach about saving the rainforest. I'm here to investigate the impact of logging and mining operations. But you? Who? I mean how?"

The old white man stood up and approached them with his arms hanging straight down along his sides. "Allow me to introduce myself. I'm Dr. Phillip Ryman." He then gestured toward the natives. "And these are the Cinta Larga Indians."

Deirdre jerked her head back with a pensive look on her face. "The Cinta Larga Indians? And Ryman? Did you say Ryman?" she stammered.

"Yes, I live here. I have for many years, and I help these people." He then gestured toward the regal-looking Indian standing next to him. "This is their Chief, Tobauqua."

The Chief acknowledged his introduction with a humble nod.

Dr. Ryman then leaned forward and peered into the pet carrier Deirdre clutched tightly.

She stepped back slightly as if to defend her precious cargo.

Dr. Ryman looked closer and squinted.

"Poaching parrots, are we?"

"Oh, heavens no, sir. This is my pet, Richard. I carried him here from the United States."

"You don't say," he said with a condescending smile.

The others gazed at each other—speechless.

With a look of hopeful optimism, Deirdre glanced from Dr. Ryman to Richard, and back to Dr. Ryman again. "Doctor, do you know anything about the ancient gift of healing?"

The Chief's eyes narrowed. The other Indians, who had been standing around, began jabbering and started walking toward the group with their spears.

Dr. Ryman's hair lifted on the back of his neck. "I suggest you leave. These people don't want you around. They're afraid you'll destroy what they protect."

Miguel promptly spoke up, "Senhora, take the papagaio out and show the good doctor—quickly."

She scrambled to take Richard out of the carrier and lifted his wing to expose the side of his body.

Nearby natives halted and stepped back. Their jabbering intensified. Chief Tobauqua fell to his knees.

Dr. Ryman openly stared as a rush of adrenalin tingled through his body. For a moment, his mind swirled with an inability to think. *Impossible!* "Dear God, the ... the mark of the white butterfly," he stuttered.

"The gift of healing, the mark of the white butterfly ... what does all that mean to you?" Ben asked. "What is the significance of this white butterfly marking?"

"Come into my hut. We must talk," Dr. Ryman said, motioning to the group.

Chapter 23

Clues

INSIDE THE CRAMPED HUT, Dr. Ryman took a seat by a table cluttered with medical instruments. Deirdre and Ben sat on wooden stools. Miguel and Demetrio stood while Chief Tobauqua remained motionless inside the hut entrance, arms still folded.

Dr. Ryman tapped the fingertips of his two hands together, stood up, took a few steps, pivoted, and sat down again before directing his attention toward Deirdre. "So tell me, how do you know about the gift of healing?"

Deirdre cleared her throat. "Miguel's sister in the States told me something about it, and I read about it in an old book I found at the library, but—" Deirdre dropped her jaw, and her eyes widened. "Omigosh ... the book ... Ryman!" She clutched at her chest. "That's it, the name of the person who wrote—"

"Ah yes, my great-grandfather, Charles Ryman," Dr. Ryman interrupted. "Of course, for years I never believed it. But now I will tell you things that few people know, but only because you possess a parrot these people thought they would never see again ... one that can unlock the secret."

"Whaddya mean?" Ben asked.

"Hundreds of years ago there was a medicine man named Ubjara who healed sick children of these Cinta Larga people, but only because his companion parrot carried the gift."

Deirdre and Ben glanced at each other and nodded.

Dr. Ryman went on. "Legend has it that after Ubjara's death, his grave became a means of continuing the gift of healing for whomever owns a descendant of his special parrot."

"Yes, and I believe I have a descendant. So, if I find the gift, I'll be able to heal sick children. Right?" Deirdre asked.

Tobauqua quickly chimed in, "You not one of us."

"Oh no!" Deirdre rubbed her forehead and threw her hands up in frustration. "I'm not one of you? So?"

Dr. Ryman searched for the right words to explain. "What the chief means is that you are not of this tribe. According to tribal prophesy, the power to heal their children will one day be returned to a chosen one of the Cinta Larga Indians. However, it is believed that an outsider can *also* make use of the gift, but only a single time ... to heal one child."

Deirdre closed her eyes and blew out a long breath. "Phew! For a minute, I thought you were going to tell me I wouldn't be able to use the gift even if I *did* find it."

"And that certainly is a big if," Ben said. "If all this is true, surely these people must know where the grave is."

"Not quite. After Ubjara's burial, a great earthquake changed the land. We know only that it is located in a magic garden hidden on top of or behind a great mountain among many mountains. Some white men have come looking for it without luck. I have heard about some who even thought they found the mountain, but there was no way to climb it. But you have the parrot."

"So how in the heck can a parrot help us to climb the mountain?"

Dr. Ryman shook his head. "Can't say I know the answer to that."

"How did your great grandfather know and how do you know all this, and how will Richard take on the healing power?" Deirdre asked.

Dr. Ryman looked over at Tobauqua. "Chief?"

Tobauqua stepped forward. "My grandfather spoke of this. His grandfathers spoke of it. Many seasons passed. No see winged one of the white butterfly."

"But surely there must be other Blue-fronted Amazon parrots around that are descendants of the medicine man's companion," Ben suggested.

Dr. Ryman shook his head. "Like the chief said, none have been seen, not for hundreds of years actually. Probably all died, unless—"

Miguel put a finger to his lips and waved it in front of himself. "Unless somewhere along the way one or more of them were poached and taken to the States."

Dr. Ryman nodded in agreement. "Anyway, the gift is locked in a tree that grew out of the medicine man's grave ... so it is said."

"Winged one with white butterfly know," Tobauqua added. "Winged one take power."

"Much of this is making sense to me now," Deirdre said. "The book in the library showed a tree with flame-like branches. Is that where the gift is located?"

"Butterflies guard tree. Butterflies know what is good ... what is evil."

Ben turned to Tobauqua. "You're talking in riddles. How on earth could little butterflies protect anything? And what about the branches that look like flames?"

"That is tree of fire. He who is evil find fire."

"You mean they would get burned if they touch it?"

"Maybe then. Maybe later."

"Brother! Can't we get a straight answer out of this guy?"

"Look, I don't know a lot about these trees," Dr. Ryman said. "The important thing is, without your parrot, you can't find or make use of the healing gift."

"Oh great, all we have to do is find a mountain we can't climb and a tree among a million trees out there. Wait until I try to teach about this in my class. The students and Dean Haase will think I've lost my mind for sure."

"You no worry if you do no evil," the Chief said.

Ben scratched his head. "If we want to find this so-called magical garden, I guess we'd better get going."

Dr. Ryman extended his arm with the palm of his hand facing up. "You are welcome to spend the night here if you wish."

Deirdre glanced over at Miguel.

"Senhora, we have plenty of daylight left. Perhaps we should keep moving."

"Yes, good idea."

* * *

After emerging from the hut, Deirdre motioned toward the tribal members.

"But won't these people wanna take Richard from me to find the gift and use it for themselves?"

Dr. Ryman glanced at the Chief, then at Richard in the pet carrier. "They wish they could. But this parrot is your companion, not the companion of any of this tribe. You, and only you, can use the gift."

Tobauqua put his hand on Deidre's shoulder. "Find gift, use wisely, then soul rests. Go now."

Dr. Ryman added, "What he means is the soul of their ancient medicine man will be freed and will find peace."

Miguel stepped forward and looked around. "I knew how to come this far, but where do we go from here?"

"And how will we know which is the right tree?" Deirdre asked.

Tobauqua pointed toward a ghostly-looking mountain range. A peculiar mist crept along the mountaintops making it difficult to tell one peak from the other. They all stood still and stared in that direction.

"Looks like only a couple of miles," Miguel said.

"You must have crossed a stream to get here. You'll have to go back that way," Dr. Ryman said.

"But the chief pointed that way," Miguel said, pointing toward the mountain range.

"The only way you can get there is along the stream. For centuries, these people occupied this entire valley. But now the other side of the stream is forbidden land."

"Land that white men took away with loud noises," Tobauqua added. "The work of the devil."

"Chain saws and bulldozers," Ben said, while nodding affirmatively. "I believe you're right, Chief."

"Follow water," Tobauqua said. He then motioned toward Richard in the pet carrier. "Your winged one will know. He carries the mark of the white butterfly. There will be clues. The messenger from above will guide him."

"Clues? A messenger? What do you mean?" Deirdre asked.

"You and your winged one will know."

Dr. Ryman waved his hand dismissively. "Off with you. Soon the rains will come making travel treacherous. Farewell, and may God be with you."

* * *

As they started to walk away, Tobauqua gently tapped Deirdre's arm. She stopped and turned. He reached in a small leather pouch on his waist and pulled out a braided bracelet from which two gold charms dangled; one shaped like a butterfly, and the other like three twisted prongs. He handed the bracelet to her.

"This Ubjara's. My grandfather give to me. His grandfather give to him. Take. You may need."

Deirdre shook her head. "No, no, I can't accept this. It must have great sentimental value for you."

"The souls of my ancestors would wish it so because you are here with your winged one. I know only that it may help you."

"I think the Chief believes that your presence here is a long-awaited prophesied mission," Dr. Ryman said.

Deirdre stared at the bracelet, then peeked into the pet carrier and held it up for Richard to see.

"Pretty, pretty," Richard said.

An Indian boy, about nine or ten years old, dashed to Tobauqua's side.

Deirdre slipped the bracelet into her pocket. "Thank you, Chief." She looked at the young boy and stooped down to him. "And who is this cute little guy?"

"My grandson, Tiko. Tiko always with animals in forest. He looking for something, I think."

"Please, Chief, let me return the favor."

She took off the rawhide necklace Ben bought for her in the marketplace and placed it around Tiko's neck.

The little wooden butterflies dangled on his bare chest. Tiko smiled and looked up at the Chief. Tobauqua nodded, indicating approval of the offering from Deirdre.

Deirdre reached down and gave Tiko a quick hug. "I like little boys who like animals."

Tiko leaned over and peered into Richard's carrier. A tiny white dot glistened on the back of his shoulder.

Squinting at first, Deirdre's eyes widened, and she stared at Tiko's back.

Richard, who had been crunching on a treat, dropped it and stepped forward. The boy and the parrot locked eyes. At that moment, a strong, mysterious wind came out of nowhere and rustled through the trees. Palm fronds slapped together as if demanding attention and swayed sharply in the direction of the mountain range. The wind subsided as suddenly as it had appeared.

Chief Tobauqua trembled, and images of what could be flashed through his mind.

As Deirdre stepped back, Richard broke the silence. "Bye, bye."

* * *

The group waved to Dr. Ryman and the Chief and set out into the rainforest.

After slogging through thick underbrush and swampy terrain for nearly an hour, Miguel, with the others following, paused near the bank of the stream they had crossed earlier. He pointed upstream. "Dr. Ryman and the Chief said we have to go that way."

Demetrio nodded and threw down a cigar butt.

As they headed upstream, their boots left deep impressions in the mud.

Chapter 24

The Reverend and His Men

ASHES DRIFTED into the air as Reverend James stirred a stick through the charred remains of a campfire. He dropped the stick, pulled out a handkerchief, and wiped his forehead.

Luis inspected trampled vegetation to one side of the campsite. He motioned to the Reverend. "They were here, senhor." He nodded toward the disturbed underbrush. "This way."

Reverend James tucked away his handkerchief. "Luis, go ahead. We'll be right behind you."

With Luis leading, they turned and trudged into the dense jungle.

* * *

Nearby, two Indian teens, brother and sister, wandered through the countryside chatting and giggling. While the boy stopped and began picking berries, the Indian girl continued on to a pond and started gathering flowers.

Rays of sunshine filtered through the trees and sparkled on the tranquil water's surface. As she knelt down admiring her reflection in the calm pool, a gold medallion, about two inches in diameter, gleamed from a thin leather band around her neck. Unexpectedly, the reflection of a man's face appeared in the water next to hers. She jerked around and started to scream, but Filipe's hand covered her mouth.

The boy dropped the berries and ran in the direction of the muffled scream. He stopped, crouched behind a bush, and peered through the vegetation.

Filipe dragged the trembling girl away from the pond, her screams muted by his tight grip over her mouth. With Luis close behind, Reverend James swaggered over and set his eyes on her neck. He gripped and caressed the gold medallion.

"Well, well. What have we here?" he said smiling widely. "Whaddya know, I believe this is solid gold." He yanked the medallion from her neck.

Derk put his hands up in disgust and backed away shuddering.

Filipe held the young girl as Reverend James continued to gloat over the medallion.

The boy, hoping not to be seen, squirmed and peeked from behind nearby bushes. He turned and started to run for help.

Luis glanced toward the sound of the rustling bushes. "What was that? Somebody was there."

The boy stopped and hid behind a tree.

Derk ran over to Filipe and grabbed him by the arm. "Let'er go. We better get outta here. Whatever village she's from can't be far away."

Filipe drew his hand away from the young girl's mouth and released her.

Seeing his sister running away from the men, the Indian boy waited for her.

Shaking uncontrollably, she sprinted into the forest, met up with her brother, and together they dashed back toward their village.

* * *

Reverend James shoved the medallion into his backpack.

"Geeze, you scared her so much she was too frightened to scream as she ran away," Derk said. He turned in the opposite direction, away from the pond area, and motioned with his arm. "Let's go."

Reverend James darted off behind Derk with Luis and Filipe close behind.

The four men disappeared into the forest.

Later, as the late afternoon sun started casting long shadows, Luis stopped along the shore of the stream and glanced down at the ground. A discarded cigar caught his eye. He stooped down, picked up the cigar, raised it up to his face, and rolled it in his fingers. Upon scanning the surrounding area, he fixed his eyes on footprints in the mud marking a trail upstream. Turning his head in that direction, he faced the mountains covering the horizon. "It looks like they head to those mountains."

Derk started to cross the stream. Up to his knees in water, he turned. "C'mon, let's get the hell outta here."

The Reverend pointed toward the mountains. "No. Luis said they headed up that way. We've got to keep following them."

"Are you crazy?" Derk said. "If that girl's tribe catches up to us they'll—"

Reverend James waded into the stream and stared directly into Derk's eyes. "Perhaps you forgot what we came here for." He then pulled out his handkerchief, dabbed his nose, and nodded toward Luis and Filipe. "Now ... me and Cheech and Chong over there are heading upstream toward those mountains with or without you. You'll never find your way back alone. So, if you wanna get home to see that lovely Alicia of yours again, I suggest you stick with us."

With Luis and Filipe following, the Reverend stomped out of the water and proceeded upstream. Derk, left standing alone in the water, jerked his head in disgust, slogged back to shore, and tagged along in a lackluster stride.

* * *

The boy and his sister arrived at their village frantically waving their arms. They rushed up to their father who, unlike the other Indian men, displayed a distinct bright red stripe down the left side of his face.

After listening to his son tell about the white men who assaulted his daughter and stole her gold medallion, the Indian father gritted his teeth and balled his fists. The veins in his neck visibly throbbed as he turned to villagers, yelling in native tongue. With bow and arrow in hand, he immediately led several Indian men into the forest.

Chapter 25

Richard's Instincts Kick In

SEVERAL HOURS passed since Deirdre, Ben, Miguel, and Demetrio left the village where they met Dr. Ryman and Tobauqua. Becoming weary, they stopped to rest. Deirdre sat down on a log and set Richard's pet carrier on the ground.

Richard's little voice rose from within his carrier, "Mommy, gotta eat."

Deirdre let Richard out of his carrier and fed him snacks. He crunched away on the food, abruptly dropped it, turned his head upward, and appeared to stare into the trees.

"Whaddya see, Richard?" Deirdre asked.

Richard unexpectedly spread his wings, took flight, and disappeared into the forest canopy.

Deirdre gasped, put her hands on her hips and peered upward. "Richard, where are you? Come to Mommy." Seeing no sign of him, her voice turned urgent. "Richard, come to Mommy." Pacing, and with her heart racing, panic sirens went off inside her. She called for Richard repeatedly.

Ben looked up and joined in. "Richard, stop fool'n around. Wait, I think I see him."

A white dove fluttered away from a tree branch.

"Just a dove," Ben said.

Deirdre's senses heightened. "A dove? A white dove?"

"Yeah, so? Does that mean something to you?"

"I'm not sure. Maybe."

* * *

High above in a kapok tree, towering at least a hundred feet, and slightly beyond where anybody could see, Richard perched next to another Blue-fronted Amazon parrot. They sat, side-by-side, on a limb above a cavity in the trunk of the tree. They affectionately preened each other and nuzzled and nibbled at each other's beaks.

It appeared Richard found a girlfriend, and he verbalized the first thing that came to his mind. "Pretty, pretty."

* * *

That evening, a fire flickered at a campsite. Sitting on the ground, Deirdre hung her head in anguish over the possibility of losing her beloved Richard.

Demetrio sat on a log smoking a cigar as usual. Miguel emerged from the trees and tossed wood on the fire.

Ben put his arms around Deirdre. "Maybe instinct has overcome Richard. This rainforest—"

She put her arms around her legs and drew them up to her chest. "But he always flies back to me." Her throat tightened. "Always! I should have never brought him here."

"He's so attached to you. I'm sure he will come back. But if for some reason he doesn't, perhaps he'll be happier here. After all, this is his true home."

She glared at Ben. "Don't you remember what Woody said? Richard would never survive in the wild. I wanted Richard to be with me forever."

"Forever? What about me?"

"Oh, of course, Ben, you too. But, well, you know, it's different for a pet, and Richard was special. I never thought I could love a pet like that, let alone a pet bird."

Ben took his hand and brushed a tear from her cheek. "Richard really does love you. I still think he might come back."

"But if he doesn't, there's no sense in going on to look for the gift of healing. It's of no use without him. And poor Penny …. You still don't believe there is such a thing anyway, do you?"

"Let's get some sleep. We'll decide what to do in the morning." That night, Ben slept off and on while holding Deirdre.

Deirdre felt some solace at his apparent attempt to comfort her. But her hope of finding Richard seemed as dim as the light of the small lantern that glimmered on his pet carrier. Thinking the worst, she focused on its emptiness and raised her eyes upward.

Where is he? Did I lose my darling Richard? Oh, Richard, please come back to Mommy.

She tried to sleep, but tossed and turned all night, imagining that the voices of the night creatures carried the voice of Richard as well.

* * *

As the morning sun touched the treetops, a thick fog clung to distant mountains.

Ben awoke and found himself alone in the tent. He stepped outside to find Deirdre staring into the jungle canopy. Miguel and Demetrio had already started to pack up their gear.

Ben put his arm around her waist. "No sign of him?"

Deirdre just kept staring into the trees without answering.

Miguel approached Ben. "Well? What now?"

Ben shook his head. "I don't think Deirdre is willing to accept that Richard may have abandoned her in favor of the rainforest that called to him. I don't know what we can do. I guess we turn back."

All packed up, they started to leave their campsite. Ben's attempt at consoling Deirdre went unrecognized. She simply shuffled along as if in a daze.

They scoured the trees as they walked, but several birds flew about from tree to tree, making it nearly impossible to distinguish if any of them could possibly be Richard.

The birds of the rainforest, always most active in the morning, squawked and called out to each other.

This morning was no different. No different except for one completely out-of-place sound that echoed faintly from the forest.

"Mommy!"

Deirdre stopped in her tracks, turned, and jerked her head upward.

"Ben, did you hear that?"

Ben stopped and listened, but only shrugged his shoulders and shook his head. "What? Hear what? Sweetheart, now I think you're hearing things."

Once again, a voice not typical of the jungle rang out.

"Mommy!"

This time Ben turned his head toward the trees. Deirdre and the others looked up. There sat Richard perched high on the limb of a palm tree.

Deirdre's face brightened.

Miguel spun around, eyes bulging, pointed toward the tree, and shouted, "Bushmaster!"

Further down the tree, a bushmaster snake slithered upward toward Richard.

Deirdre looked downward chillingly. The look on her face transformed from one of joy to one of terror. She grabbed on to Ben and shouted, "Oh my God. Richard, come to Mommy."

Seemingly unaware of the impending danger, Richard calmly preened himself, acting as if he was in no hurry to go anywhere. Deirdre stared in horror as the slinking reptile approached Richard. Within inches of the unaware parrot, the menacing snake closed in and drew its head back into a striking pose.

All four of them called out, "Richard, go to Mommy. Richard, fly ... fly to Mommy."

"Richard, come to Mommy, *now*," Deirdre yelled.

Just as the snake motioned to strike, Richard flew off the branch and glided down to Deirdre's outstretched arm.

"Hi, Mommy. Are you okay?" Richard said calmly.

Deirdre smiled widely and breathed a shaky sigh of relief. "Oh, Richard, don't you ever do that again. Yes, I'm okay."

The group watched as the snake slithered away.

"Well, I guess this means we go on, doesn't it?" Ben declared.

Deirdre smiled at Richard and asked him, "Richard, do you wanna continue?"

"Yeah," he replied.

She kissed him and placed him safely back into his pet carrier.

The group continued upstream.

Ben stopped for a moment and peered up at the ghostly mountain range ahead. A feeling of uncertainty crept up his spine. *Omigosh, what are we getting ourselves in to.*

Chapter 26

A Defining Moment

THE HOT SUN beat down on them later that day, so they stopped by a stream pool to rest, cool off, and grab a bite to eat. An eerie mist hovered over huge mountains towering before them.

Deirdre stepped out of her khakis and waded into deep water to bathe while Ben washed up in the shallows.

Demetrio stole a quick peek at Deirdre's near-naked body and smiled as he and Miguel munched on some food.

A short time later, Ben and Deirdre emerged from the pool, dried off and dressed.

With a tension-filled expression, Ben looked across the stream and up at the mountain range. He fidgeted, ran his hand through his hair, and then put his arms around Deirdre. "Dee, we've been here for days. I almost drowned in a river. Some Indians scared the wits out of us. You almost lost Richard. I still find this cockamamie story about some gift of healing hard to believe. Be happy that you got your Richard back. I'd like to spend a little more time talking to Pete back at the logging site, and then maybe we should think about heading home."

"I'm not ready to give up so easily." Deirdre paced in a circle holding her forehead. "Oh, I don't know ... maybe you're right. Dr. Ryman and the Chief talked about clues, but even Miguel doesn't know where to go from here. And I'd rather not put both you and Richard through—"

Deidre tilted her head to the side and stared, focusing her attention on Ben's chest.

A small white butterfly, wings softly fluttering, rested on his shirt. Then one settled on his nose. He shooed it away. Several more landed on his shirt. Out of nowhere, more and more white butterflies appeared, one after the other.

Deirdre continued in a stuttering tone. "Rather not ... put ... put Richard—"

"What? What is it?" Ben asked.

At first, just a few white butterflies fluttered, but soon, hundreds surrounded them and converged onto their clothing.

Miguel and Demetrio ogled at the pearly creatures swarming about.

Bouncing from foot to foot, Deirdre called out, "Ben, look. Look around. White butterflies ... that's it ... a sign! Richard must have attracted them so that they can lead the way. The magic garden can't be far from here."

The flurry of a few hundred soon transformed into a blizzard of snowy insects. They soared all around them as far as the eye could see, gradually evolving into an enchanting pathway leading directly toward the tall mountain.

Led by Deirdre walking briskly and then breaking into a jog, they followed the meandering trail of swirling butterflies. The faint sound of rushing water intensified as they got closer to the mountain. Soon they spotted a narrow and magnificent waterfall cascading down over a hundred feet from a cliff into a pool below.

Deirdre stopped, held her breath, covered her mouth with her hand, and stared.

"What?" Ben asked.

Exhaling while she peered up, she said, "That's the waterfall I saw in the book. We're real close. I'm certain."

"It's just a waterfall. How in the world can you possibly know it's the one you saw in the book?"

"I know it is. I just know it." She reached into the pet carrier, and Richard stepped up onto her hand.

Miguel and Demetrio stumbled up to her side. "Senhora, now what?" Miguel asked.

"Chief Tobauqua said that my winged one would know ... and I believe him." Appearing relaxed, she looked down at Richard perched on her hand, and gave an easy nod. "Yes, *he* will know."

Chapter 27

The Mysterious Ascending Cave

AN ENORMOUS, ROCKY cliff rose high into the sky before Deirdre and the others as they followed the trail of butterflies to the bank of a river flowing along the base of the mountain.

The river, about thirty yards wide, looked to be only two or three feet deep. The far side splashed along the base of the vertical rock face of the mountain and bounced angrily around a car-sized boulder near the middle of the river. Where Deirdre's group stood, the river carved out a steep, muddy bank, showing a high watermark several feet above the current water level.

A mood of dread and hopelessness pervaded as they stood in silence and gaped at the wall of sheer rock.

Deirdre shook her head and shuddered as she peered across the river and up along the cliff.

Richard, sitting on her shoulder, acted jittery. His head jerked around and tilted upward as if someone or something summoned him.

Miguel peered up and down the river and scrubbed a hand over his face. "Senhora, it looks like we hit a dead end. All I see on the other side of the river is the mountain. It is just gray rock straight up." Shielding his eyes from the sun and looking up toward the mountaintop, he continued, "I see two openings way up there. One is near the top." With eyes squinting, he then raised his arm and pointed. "Look! The butterflies ... they fly up there, and it looks like they fly in and out of that upper opening."

Ben tipped his head to one side. "Could that possibly be the entrance to the so-called magic garden? It's impossible to get up there. There's no way we could climb up that rock face."

Without warning, Richard abruptly took off from Deirdre's shoulder and flew toward the cliff.

Deirdre sucked in a quick breath. Watching in horror as Richard fluttered into the sky, she shouted, "Richard! Oh no, not again!"

Richard flew upward until he became a mere shadow blending in with the butterflies. He then disappeared into the opening near the top of the mountain.

That instant, an earsplitting *rumble* emanated from the cliff directly across the river and caught the group's attention. The ground shook, and they watched with widening eyes as a door-sized slab of rock separated from the cliff just above water level and shifted out of the riverbed straight up along the cliff. Then as if on a track, the slab slid to the left and scraped across the rocky surface. As it grinded its way to the side, it left a trail of pebbles and dust in its wake and slowly revealed a gap in the cliff barely above water level. Water surged in and out of the cave-like opening, repeatedly sucking it up and spitting it out.

Deirdre clamped her hands to her chest.

Miguel waded a few feet into the river and turned to Ben. "Senhor, I cannot believe my eyes. Do you see that? Part of the cliff ... it opens like a door."

With a slow, disbelieving shake of the head, Ben stepped back and peered up at the top of the mountain. "Omigod, it was Richard. Do you suppose—"

Wading further into the water, Miguel called back to the others, "Yes, for sure. What are we waiting for? Let's go."

Trembling, Deirdre moved one hand to her stomach and grabbed Ben's arm with the other. "I don't know. That cave entrance looks awfully small."

Ben gave a darting gaze across the river. "That cave may look small to you, but this river looks pretty wide to me."

Miguel glanced back and forth. "The cave, it looks small? The stream is wide? But that looks like the way into the mountain. Your papagaio is in there somewhere. That is where we must go to find what you came here for."

Facing Deirdre, Ben rubbed his hand behind his head. "I'm not crazy about going in there either, but sweetheart, Miguel is right. Richard is inside that mountain."

With lips pressed together, Deirdre's anxiety transformed into an uncanny calmness. Extreme mental focus on her objective took over. With a curt nod and an alert gaze toward the cave, she blew out a series of short breaths. "You know, that cave doesn't look so small after all."

With Richard's empty carrier in hand, she rushed into the river nearly up to her waist, water splashing wildly.

Miguel dashed after her. "Senhora."

Ben entered the river, hesitated momentarily, then slogged his way across.

Demetrio jolted into the water and joined them.

As they approached the cave, the channel deepened. Miguel grabbed Deirdre's arm and took over the lead.

Chest-high in water, they slowly waded through the cave entrance and far into the dark and dank grotto. Eventually they sloshed out of the wet passage and stepped up onto a dry ledge inside.

Although some sunlight entered the cave, Miguel pulled out a flashlight and pointed it straight ahead. The light hit a cave wall. He then directed the beam of light up above his head. "It seems to end here, but I see a small opening above me. Looks like it leads to another passageway."

Miguel and Demetrio squeezed their way straight up through the tight, rocky shaft, which opened up into a spacious cavern.

Ben started to push Deirdre up through the opening, but her breathing became rapid and raspy. Demetrio grabbed her hand, and with one swift movement, jerked her up through the shaft. Ben then followed.

Deirdre brushed off her clothing and took a deep breath of the stagnant, musty air. "Wow, this is almost as big as our house." A tiny hairclip fell off her head onto the cave floor. She took a step and heard a *crunch*. "Oh heck." She reached down and picked up one of the pieces.

"Don't worry about that thing," Ben said. "We need to get oriented."

Miguel shined the flashlight all around. "It looks like there's only one way to go from here—up."

The group slowly started making their way along the passageway that gradually sloped upward. The cave widened and took on the appearance of a grand cathedral. Anomalous rocky outcrops, stalactites, and stalagmites flourished. Light filtering down from the upper reaches of the cave took on brilliant colors as it reflected off the cave walls comprised of a multitude of rock formations. Ledges and pathways spiraled in front of them.

Mesmerized, Deirdre stared in awe at the beauty of this natural geological wonder. "Whoooa!" She then called out, "Richard!" Her voice echoed loudly through the cavern. She turned to Ben. "He's got to be up there somewhere."

Miguel and Demetrio led the way through the scenic labyrinth. They climbed up steep ledges still lugging gear. The air became thin and stale. Their voices echoed through the cavern every time one of them spoke. Even the sound of their breathing resounded through the enigmatic hollow.

* * *

Surveying the cave walls along the way, Ben paused to inspect rocks. "That's odd."

The others stopped.

Ben continued, "We're inside a huge mountain, and yet these geological formations don't make sense. I see several different rock structures. Mostly an unusual combination of sedimentary rock ... looks like compressed sediment and clay. But I also see some metamorphic granite and quartzite, and even some igneous gneiss." Inspecting the cave walls further, he focused on one area in particular. "Miguel, hand me that light a second."

As Ben shined the light onto the cave wall, the silhouette of a human figure, as if lying on a bed, came into view. Moving the light, another silhouette appeared, then another, and another.

"What do you make of this, Senhor Ben?" Miguel asked.

"Actually, looks like bodies in burial positions. Indians maybe."

Ben dug out his camera and snapped a picture.

Deirdre leaned toward the cave wall, squinted, and peered at the head of one of the body figures. The eye appeared to move and wink at her. She jumped back and squealed.

As Ben looked closer, a small object crawled out of a hole in the rock and scurried away. "A spider, just a spider," he said, chuckling.

"Could this be some sort of ancient burial ground?" Deirdre asked.

Miguel shook his head. "The local Indians ... they bury their dead in the ground, not in a mountain cave."

Deirdre walked in a tight circle dabbing her fingers over her mouth. "But supposedly hundreds of years ago there was some kind of cataclysmic earthquake in this area after the tribe buried Ubjara, the medicine man. Right?"

"That's it," Ben added. "All this was once underground. The earthquake could have heaved up the burial ground to form this mountain. That might explain these odd rock formations."

* * *

Meanwhile, with Luis leading, Reverend James and his men, who had been following closely behind, approached the river at the base of the mountain.

Luis looked down at footprints and peered across at the cave entrance. "There's no other place for them to go, chefe. They must have gone into that cave across the river."

Reverend James surveyed the area, scratched his chin and nodded. "Mmm, must be. Let's take a look." He then motioned to cross.

Filipe pulled out a large knife.

"Put that away, you fool," Derk ordered.

The men proceeded across the river to the cave entrance.

Once inside, with flashlight in hand, Luis led them up into the cavern. He stopped, noticed something shining on the cave floor, reached down, and picked it up.

The Reverend snatched it out of his hand, inspected the broken piece of hairclip, and peered into the shadowy cavern ahead. "I'd say we're on the right track."

Chapter 28

Finding Their Way

PUZZLING ROCK formations surrounded Demetrio as they continued upward through the winding, cavernous maze. The group knew only that Richard had flown into an opening somewhere high above as though directed by an unseen force.

While they continued discussing possible explanations for the existence of this mysterious mountain and the cave within it, the clatter of falling pebbles echoed through the cavern.

Startled, Demetrio turned his attention toward the direction of the sound coming from the lower cave area.

"What is it?" Miguel asked.

"I thought I heard something below."

They froze and glanced at each other.

Miguel shined a flashlight at small lizards scurrying across the cave wall. "Just cave critters, I guess."

With Demetrio leading, they pressed on. He stopped abruptly, and Miguel almost stumbled into him. Ben and Deirdre, who lagged slightly behind, caught up. Deirdre took a deep breath.

"What's up?" Ben asked.

"Look … it goes two ways. It goes up." He then motioned his head to the right. "It goes that way to the side, too."

"Yeah, so!" Deirdre exclaimed. "Richard flew through the opening at the top of the mountain. If we go over that way, we may lose him. We need to keep going up."

Ben peered over at the side passageway. "But look, I see light over that way."

"He's right," Demetrio said to Miguel while stretching his neck to the right. "There *is* light down there. We check it out."

Miguel nodded and followed Demetrio into the narrow, side passageway.

Ben shrugged his shoulders, grabbed Deirdre's hand, and they tagged along behind Miguel.

As they tiptoed deeper into the unknown, it gradually became brighter. Eventually they found themselves standing at the base of a long, narrow canyon. Sunlight entered from the mountain's surface hundreds of feet above. Looking straight ahead, they saw the canyon was about twenty yards wide with ninety-degree cliffs on both sides towering straight up above them. To their left and right, the canyon seemed to meander endlessly in both directions.

Demetrio bent his head backward and, with eyes squinting, looked straight up at the sky. "If we must go way up there, it sure looks like we no get there from here." Pointing across to the other side of the canyon, he went on, "But look, the passageway ... it goes on over there. Let's follow it. I want to see what is there."

Ben and Deirdre looked up at the sky in awe as they followed behind Miguel and Demetrio. The passageway once again evolved into darkness.

"Give us some light," Deirdre called out, breathing heavily.

After Demetrio and Miguel turned on their flashlights, Ben fumbled to turn on his.

The beam of light from Demetrio's flashlight shined straight ahead and illuminated a large mass of thick roots. "What the—" He took a few more steps forward, turned, and came back to the others. "This is as far as we go here. Up ahead, those roots, they block the passageway."

"We need to go back to the main cave that goes up," Miguel said.

Demetrio and Miguel headed back in the direction from which they came.

Deirdre followed for a moment, but stopped and turned to Ben, who continued to focus his attention on a wall of the narrow cave with his flashlight. "Hey! Indiana! C'mon, we're going back."

"Wait. Look at this."

Demetrio and Miguel scrambled back to where Ben stood.

Ben shined his light on another skeletal profile of a human figure etched in the cave wall. He slowly moved his flashlight upward from the figure and then over to the mass of roots at the end of the passageway.

They all gawked at the figure in the wall.

"I guess this is part of old Indian graveyard, huh?" Demetrio suggested.

"Yeah," Ben said. "But those roots are growing right out of the body of this Indian."

Deirdre eyed the outline and took in a deep breath. "Chief Tobauqua said the gift is locked in a tree that grew out of the medicine man's grave. Remember?"

Without saying a word, they all gaped once again at the Indian outline in the cave wall. They then exchanged knowing glances.

Deirdre's eyes widened. "Could this be—"

Miguel looked up with a blank stare and finished her question. "Ubjara? Yes, senhora, I believe so."

Ben pointed. "Looks like the roots keep growing in that direction, but Demetrio is right ... we can't go any farther that way. If we can ever find our way to the top of this mountain, maybe we'll find the tree those roots belong to."

"And hopefully we'll find Richard up there too." Deirdre rushed her words. "C'mon, let's go. We need to find him."

With Miguel now in the lead, they headed back toward the main cave.

* * *

As Reverend James and his men approached the area where the side passage split off from the main cavern, voices resonated from within.

Luis stopped and put his hand up, halting Filipe, Derk, and Reverend James in their tracks. "Shhh, quick, hide."

They bolted behind a wall of rock just as Deirdre's group, with Miguel in front, exited the side passageway and turned to continue up the main cavern.

"Wait here, 'til they're far enough ahead," the Reverend whispered.

Chapter 29

Daylight

A GLISTENING, ROCKY, spiral stairway weaved its way upward taking the group out of the main cavern and into a passageway leading to the upper area of the cave. Occasionally, they came across narrow ledges forcing them to step sideways to ensure safe access to the area above. The farther up they went, the easier it became to see and distinguish objects. The shadowy passageway gradually gave way to a moderately lit grotto.

Ben felt fresh air drifting his way. After he stumbled and climbed up a ledge, a ray of sunlight hit his face. Slipping and almost falling, he rushed to a door-sized opening in the cave wall leading to the outside. Pebbles tumbled off the edge and seemed to take forever before they splashed into the water below. His eyes widened.

The others rushed over to the ledge and caught deep breaths of the fresh air. Pausing for a moment, Ben admired the view of the distant rainforest, the mountains and valleys, the nearby waterfall, and the river below.

Ben quickly reached in his backpack and pulled out his camera. "Magnificent," he said as he snapped pictures. "I can't wait to lecture about this in class."

Clouds as black as a Halloween cat gathered on the horizon and reached for the ground. Thunder rumbled in the distance. The scent of rain crossed Ben's nose.

While walking back into the upper cavern, Ben and Demetrio stopped, turned, and gave one last glance at the threatening sky. Ben squinted. Demetrio gave a hesitant nod.

Deirdre plopped down like a rag doll on a small rocky ledge. "What if Richard isn't up there? What if something happened to him?" She called out, "Richard!"

Ben stooped down in front of her and took her hand. "We'll find him. I promise. Miguel, we need to take a rest. Deirdre's exhausted."

After dropping his gear, Demetrio leaned on a ledge.

Miguel sat on the cave floor, crossed his legs, and clasped his hands together. A moment later, he stood up and ran his hand through his hair. "Two openings ... there were two openings."

Demetrio turned his head. "Huh?"

"When we looked up at this mountain, I saw two openings, not far apart. The papagaio ... he fly into the upper one. This is the first opening we came to, so the other one must be up there somewhere." He pointed upward.

Ben got to his feet. "That's right, and it can't be much farther ahead."

Deirdre rose, exhaled, and gazed toward the passageway above them.

As the group climbed higher into the shadowy, spiral-shaped corridor of the cave, white butterflies reappeared glowing like fireflies. More daylight shimmered from above, suggestive of another window to the outside. Fresh air drifted across their faces.

Pointing to the second opening, Miguel turned to Deirdre. "Look. That must be it … the opening on the side of the mountain your papagaio fly into. It looks like the cave ends here. I think we are inside the top of this mountain."

Deirdre scanned the area calling, "Richard! Richard!"

They scrambled to the side opening at the summit.

Deirdre spun frantically around with darting eyes. "Yes, this is where he flew in. I'm sure."

More glowing white butterflies flew about.

Ben turned around and fixed his eyes on a stream of butterflies radiating from the other side of the cave.

"Maybe he flew back out," Deirdre said. "Where is he?" Grabbing at fistfuls of her hair, she continued calling, "Richard!"

Everyone stood still as a single green feather floated silently down past Deirdre's face. Without moving, her eyes followed the feather down to the cave floor. She then slowly lifted her gaze.

From far above, came a small, childlike voice, "Mommy!"

Deirdre jolted around and peered upward. High up on a ledge perched Richard, casually preening himself.

"There you are. Come to Mommy."

Richard fluttered obediently to Deirdre's shoulder.

Ben grinned, but then turned his attention toward the butterflies he spied at the other side of the cave. He sauntered away from the others. A bright ray of light slid across his face as he came to another narrow passageway leading to the outside. Sunbeams widened across his body. He gawked at the landscape outside the cave and felt his face break into a wide smile.

Sucking in a quick breath while waving to the others, he shouted, "Hey, com'ere, wait'll you see this."

Chapter 30

The Magic Garden

THE STRANGE LAND before them exhibited an odd combination of beauty and ghastliness like nothing Deirdre had ever seen. Staring bewilderedly, she slowly inched her way out of the cave. She treaded cautiously, as if dazed, and glanced at the others to see if they all experienced the same amazement.

Ben reached for Deirdre's hand, and they tiptoed into a meadow of green grass, flowering vegetation, and weird trees of all sizes and shapes. Spindly branches protruded from the trees, all with oddly-shaped leaves colored red, yellow, purple, and other radiant shades. Grass and flowering bushes sprouted up among the trees. Thousands of white butterflies danced about flowers of every color imaginable.

At a loss for words, and at first hesitating, Deirdre gripped Ben's hand tightly, then stepped forward. With a slow disbelieving shake of her head, she gazed out at the mysterious terrain.

Richard, on Deirdre's shoulder, jerked his head around as if surveying the landscape. "Pretty, pretty," he said.

Miguel slowly pivoted his head from side to side. "*Lindo maravilhoso pra caramba!*"

Ben turned to Miguel and gave him a blank look. "Huh?"

"Let's just say, I think this land is beautiful."

Soon the group came upon a deep canyon. Although only about twenty yards wide, it looked as if it went on endlessly in both directions.

Ben walked close to the edge and peered down into the depths of the abyss. "Ya know what this is? This is that narrow valley we stood in way down below along that smaller passageway. We're now at the top."

Reaching across the canyon, a peculiar arrangement of thick gnarly roots intertwined to form a crude bridge.

Ben scanned the landscape on the other side. "How can this be? We're on top of a mountain, and yet there are cliffs all around. When we stood in front of the mountain below, we couldn't see that this land ... this kingdom, existed behind it."

"This place must have been made by the great earthquake," Miguel added.

Deirdre stepped forward. "This is it ... the magic garden. The gift of healing must be here somewhere. But the trees ... there's so many of them."

Miguel pointed across the canyon. "The roots we saw down below, they grew in that direction. The tree you look for must be on other side of canyon."

"Yes, of course," Ben said. "No matter what, I definitely wanna see what's over there." He pressed one foot onto the vine entanglement.

Demetrio reached out to him. "Wait, let me go."

Ben stepped back.

Demetrio casually lit a cigar, blew a spiraling puff of smoke into the air, and stepped onto the vine bridge. It swayed back and forth as he proceeded across with cautious steps. Once on the other side, he waved to the others. "Come, it is safe to cross."

Ben held Deirdre's hand tightly. The bridge sagged and the roots squeaked and groaned ominously as they crossed. A root snapped at the edge of the cliff, but the bridge held. Miguel crossed last.

Speechless, wide-eyed, and overwhelmed, they made their way through the strange land. White butterflies swirled around them. Menacing black clouds continued to gather in the distant sky.

Upon reaching the side of a steep rocky cliff, they gazed up in awe at a white fuzzy cigar-shaped column, about ten-foot-wide, attached to the side of the rock face. It towered fifty feet or more up along the side of the cliff.

Demetrio approached the odd column. He poked his finger into it and it made a *squishy* sound. Squinting and looking upward, his face twisted, "What is this? Some sort of giant fungus?"

As he pulled back his finger, a bulging spasm, accompanied by a *sloshing whoosh* pulsated up and down the column as if something inside became disturbed. Demetrio lurched back and yelped.

"What is it?" Ben asked.

"The thing moved. I swear. It moved."

Ben eyed up the towering column. "If I didn't know better, I'd say this is some sort of giant cocoon. But that can't be. Not something this large."

They continued to wander across a landscape of tall, unusual looking shrubs. The taller trees had leaves on the lower branches, but the higher branches hung bare. A strange pink mist hugged the ground but swirled upward in some areas like tiny twisters.

"I just noticed something odd," Ben said.

"Are you kidding me? What isn't loco about this place?" Miguel insisted.

"There are no animals. Not a squirrel, not a bird. Just these white butterflies all over the place."

"Not even a beer can or cigar butt," Demetrio added with a chuckle.

Soon they came upon a wide, solitary tree. The tree's branches and leaves, sparkling and glimmering in shades of yellow and white, swayed slowly as if made of down feathers, and yet the air showed no sign of a breeze. A drifting mist gradually cleared, revealing branching in the shape of a butterfly. In addition to a multitude of thumb-sized cocoons and two-inch white caterpillars blanketing the tree, thousands of white butterflies circled it like a white tornado.

Demetrio jerked his head to and fro dodging the white butterflies. "Senhora Dee, this must be what you look for. This tree even looks like a big butterfly."

Deirdre squinted and took a closer look. "That does make sense."

"This tree is different from the others, alright, but what makes you so sure this is the one?" Miguel asked.

"It's obviously where all those butterflies came from," Ben said.

Deirdre reached to her shoulder for Richard. He stepped onto her hand. She held him up high.

Ben grabbed her arm forcing her to lower her hand. "Dee, are you sure about this? What if this isn't the tree?"

"It's so beautiful ... this has to be it."

Miguel chimed in, "Remember what Chief Tobauqua said. Your papagaio will know."

Deirdre once again held Richard high and gave him the command she taught him back home. "Richard, tree."

Richard turned, cowered by Deirdre's neck, and whimpered like a small child.

Miguel looked up. A white dove sat on a branch of the tree, then flew off.

"I'll be ... there *are* other creatures here. At least one other bird, anyway," Miguel said, shrugging his shoulders. "Senhora, what is your papagaio afraid of? Butterflies?"

Ben gazed at the white dove as it flew into the distance. "No. Something warned Richard not to go to this tree."

"*Meu Deus*. The tree of fire," Miguel said as he crossed himself and stared fixedly at the tree.

Deirdre's mind raced through the possibilities. "What did you say?"

"The tree of fire. This must be the tree of fire!"

At first, Deirdre's thoughts were too scattered to think straight. Chief Tobauqua's words echoed in her head. *Butterflies guard tree. Butterflies know what is good … what is evil. Winged one with white butterfly know.* "Yes, yes, I think you're right, Miguel. This must be the tree of fire Chief Tobauqua spoke of. He said butterflies protect the gift of healing. What if this tree is meant to throw off intruders by mimicking a butterfly? Maybe what it's actually doing is hiding and protecting the real tree we're looking for."

Deirdre tiptoed around one side of the tree. The others followed. As they slowly circled to the other side of the tree, a mist unveiled another single, lonely-looking tree growing by itself. It stood only about twelve feet tall with thick, unsightly, knotty, mangrove-like branches.

They all stared with befuddled looks on their faces.

* * *

Meanwhile, from the lower reaches of the cave, Reverend James and his men made their way upward.

"I can't wait to get my hands on that blonde," Filipe said in a hushed tone.

Luis chuckled.

Acting jittery, Derk glanced at the two lowlifes and shook his head in disgust. With a pained expression, he grabbed Filipe, spun him around, and spoke with forced restraint. "Haven't you caused enough trouble?"

Filipe reached for his knife.

Reverend James pulled out a pistol and pointed it in the direction of all three of them. "Keep your voices down, you idiots. Settle your differences later ... after I get what I came here for."

The three men sneered at each other and, for the moment, settled down.

Flashing a chilly, insincere smile, Derk continued to follow Reverend James and the others up through the cavern.

Eventually, they reached the high point of the mountain hollow and found their way into the magic garden.

Luis put his hand up to his forehead, shielding his eyes from the sun, and scanned the landscape. Raising a set of binoculars to his eyes, he pointed across the canyon. "I see them. They are there. They just walked around behind a big feathery-looking tree."

Being careful not to be spotted, the Reverend and his men crossed the vine bridge and stealthily made their way to the area of the butterfly-shaped tree. Hiding behind it, they watched as Deirdre's group approached the lonely-looking tree.

"What the—" Reverend James said as his eyes followed Deirdre.

Chapter 31

The Transfer

WHILE PRYING EYES watched from behind the tree of fire, Deirdre, with a feeling of dread, peered at the unsightly tree with the knotty-looking branches.

Demetrio shook his head. "It doesn't look like anything is over here."

"What about that funny-looking tree there?" Ben suggested, pointing.

Demetrio simply smirked. "That ugly thing? I think that is nothing. You are wasting your time."

Miguel rubbed the back of his neck and squinted at the twisted branches as if he wasn't certain what to believe.

The white dove reappeared and sat briefly on a branch of the repulsive little tree before taking flight again.

"It won't hurt to see what Richard thinks," Deirdre said as she lifted Richard on her hand. "Richard, tree."

Deirdre shivered with expectation as Richard slowly spread his wings.

He held his wings out widely and sprang into the air in the direction of the pathetic looking tree. At first, he flapped briskly, but then his wings moved slowly, literally in slow motion. He soared through the air, pumping his wings only occasionally and gliding much of the way. Although the tree stood only about twenty yards away, it seemed to take Richard forever to reach the top branch. It was as if time stood still. He extended his legs like an eagle about to snatch its prey, landed on the branch, and tucked his wings in along his sides.

The entire group stared with rapt attention, mouths gaping.

Deirdre froze, clamped her arms around her waist, and closed her eyes in an attempt to stay calm.

At first nothing happened. Richard showed no fear of this tree like the other. He sat on the top limb, fanned his tail, shook his feathers, and cocked his head to the side just as he did at home when happy and content.

Deirdre's heart pounded.

Then in an instant, Richard's demeanor changed. Looking proud and mighty, he craned his neck and stood upright as if instinctually awaiting something. Fluffing out his feathers and tilting his head toward the sky, he screeched a primal jungle sound unlike any Deirdre had ever heard.

Miguel glanced around at the others. Then he looked down at his feet. "Something is happening. Feel that?"

Gradually the ground started to vibrate and rumble. They held on to each other, steadying themselves.

The gray sky, with low clouds, reflected a faint light resembling distant lightning. A ghostly, bright turquoise-blue glow emanated from the ground and crept up the trunk of the tree, gradually filling each branch one at a time. White butterflies flew in from all directions and encircled the tree. Richard's entire body took on the bright blue glow. The tree then burst out with a brilliant white light like an enormous flashbulb spreading hundreds of shimmering sparkles into the air. Richard's body attracted and soaked up all the sparkles like a magnet.

A time-chiseled, wrinkled face of an old man gradually appeared in a vaporous mist above Richard. A haunting voice, as if coming from nowhere and yet from everywhere, resonated.

"Use this gift wisely. My people are grateful. There will now be another like me."

While the face and the mist faded away as strangely as it appeared, Demetrio fell to his knees.

Miguel reached out toward the tree and took a deep breath. "The ghost of Ubjara."

The light in Richard's body slowly waned and receded down the tree as if sucked back down into the earth. He spread his wings and soared back to Deirdre's outstretched hand.

She drew him close to her body and hugged him. "Oh, my baby. You scared Mommy so much. Thank God you are okay. We did it, Richard." She then lifted her head toward the sky. "Hopefully you have been blessed with the gift of healing. Time to go home. I hope we're not too late." She quickly placed Richard into his pet carrier.

"We must go, senhora," Miguel said, regaining his composure. "There is little time. The clouds ... the rains. Come."

Ben took Deirdre's hand. "I wonder what he meant by 'there will now be another like me'? He must have been referring to you, sweetheart."

"Could be," Miguel said. "But remember, if your papagaio has the power, it can only be used once. So, who is it that will be like Ubjara?"

Deirdre stopped and gave Miguel a sidelong glance.

Lightning flashed, thunder boomed and black clouds rolled across the sky. Rain started to fall noisily.

Rainwater ran down Miguel's face as he yelled, "Hurry, the rains make the rivers rise quickly."

The group turned and began to make their way back around to the front of the large butterfly-shaped tree of fire.

* * *

With Derk, Filipe, and Luis by his side, Reverend James lurked near the tree trunk and chuckled smugly. "Ah, yes, they led us right to it." He pulled a gun from his belt.

As Deirdre's group appeared from behind the tree, the Reverend pointed his gun in their direction.

Deirdre and the others halted with dazed looks on their faces.

Luis circled behind Ben and grabbed him around the neck. Filipe darted up to Deirdre and, in an instant, snatched Richard's carrier from her.

"I'll take that," he said.

Deirdre screamed, and her eyes blazed with shock.

Miguel and Demetrio rushed toward Filipe, but stopped when he wielded his large knife, and Reverend James fired his gun into the ground at their feet. Filipe held on to Richard's carrier.

"Mommy," Richard cried out. "Mommy!"

Deirdre fell to the ground, reached out toward Richard's carrier, and called out hysterically. "No! Richard!"

Lightning and thunder ripped through the landscape and the rain intensified, soaking everyone. Reverend James, still aiming his gun at them, leaned comfortably against the trunk of the butterfly-shaped tree of fire. His dark eyes bored into Deirdre's as she raged.

With wide eyes, Ben and Miguel stared at him leaning against the tree.

The Reverend glared at them and glanced back at the tree, shrugged his shoulders, then moved away from it with a confident walk. "Well, well, Professor, I have to thank you and your lovely wife for finding what I need to make me rich," the Reverend said, speaking slowly in an arrogant tone.

Derk stood nearby, appearing uncomfortable. Reverend James continued to flaunt his gun at the others as the rainstorm intensified.

Ben, his face contorted in fury, struggled a bit with Luis and stretched his neck, veins bulging, toward Reverend James. "You fool. That bird won't do you any good."

"Is that so?"

Reverend James ordered Luis to let Ben go, and motioned for Derk and Filipe to start making their way back toward the cave. He continued pointing his gun at the group as he walked slowly backwards toward the canyon. They dashed across the vine bridge over the canyon.

Springing into action, Miguel and Demetrio took chase, but skidded to a halt when Reverend James fired his gun at them from the other side of the canyon. The bullet struck a nearby tree, barely missing Demetrio. Ben and Deirdre caught up to Miguel and Demetrio and stood at the edge of the canyon.

"Don't try to be heroes," Reverend James shouted back to them. "Oh, by the way, I don't need any of you anymore. I can't let you go back to the states now can I!" His voice heckled like that of a teenage neighborhood bully. "The news will read: professor and wife disappear in Brazil." He lifted his arm and waved it across the front of his body. "Nobody will find you here. If you're lucky, maybe you'll find enough food to survive in this strange land."

The Reverend turned to Filipe and pointed down at the root bridge. "Filipe, can you cut through those vines with that big knife of yours?"

"Sim, Chefe, but it will take time."

"Well, don't just stand there. Get on it."

Using his large knife, Filipe hacked at the vines coming out of the canyon wall. Derk reached down and grabbed at Filipe, but Luis pulled him off just as Filipe finished cutting through the last couple of vines. The vine bridge entanglement crashed against the far canyon wall leaving Deirdre and the others stranded with no possible way to cross the canyon and get back to the cave.

As Reverend James and his men headed toward the cave, Deirdre, Ben, Miguel and Demetrio stood on the other side of the canyon in pouring rain, water dripping down their long faces.

Reverend James saw Derk glance across the chasm and noticed the remorseful look on his face as he started toward the cave but changed direction in mid-stride. The Reverend watched with concern as Derk peered back again at the forlorn group. Turning and darting back into the cave, Derk finally joined him, Filipe, and Luis.

With Luis leading, they started downward into the interior of the cavern.

Red-faced and teeth gnashing, Derk dashed past Filipe and grabbed Reverend James. "Now you've gone too far. I didn't sign up to be part of killing innocent people."

Filipe charged at Derk, who spun around just as Filipe lunged at him with a knife. The knife cut into Derk's side. A startled look crept across Derk's face, his eyes rolled up into their sockets, and he dropped to his knees. Filipe then kicked him, and he rolled into a crevice about eight feet below where they stood. He lay limp as Filipe and Luis looked down at him.

Reverend James walked over and peered at the crumpled, once-faithful head of Church security, eyes now shut, blood running down his shirt. "Leave him. I couldn't trust him anymore anyway. He can rot here in this cave like our friends will rot on the other side of that canyon."

The three men made their way downward through the cavern. By the time they reached the cave exit, the water level had risen considerably as a result of the heavy rain. The creek at the base of the mountain nearly swallowed up the cave opening. Filipe held Richard's carrier high above his head as they waded through the rising, chest-deep water and out of the cave. They scampered out of the river and up the far-side bank. Reverend James looked back at the mountain with satisfaction before heading into the rainforest.

Luis smiled at Filipe. "Now we get paid."

Chapter 32

The Predicament

DEIRDRE PLUMMETED into despair. Rain-soaked, she sat in the mud, clawed at her cheeks, and sobbed. Her stomach churned. "This is all my fault. We're going to die here."

The driving rain made it difficult to see as Miguel gazed up and down the canyon. "There has got to be another way out."

Ben pulled Deirdre to her feet, and they started walking, the heavy raindrops still showering down on them ceaselessly like BB pellets from the sky. The group walked along the canyon in one direction, but as the rain started to ease up, they saw no end in sight. They turned around and hiked back the other way. Eventually, they stopped and rested.

"Instead of finding a way to cross canyon, maybe we walk back to the trees." Demetrio suggested. "Might be a way out on the other side of this … this place."

"But look, this plateau is completely enclosed by high cliffs," Ben said. "You're our guide, Miguel, don't you know how we can get out of here?"

"I know the rainforest. But this? This magic garden, or whatever it is way up on top of this mountain? Sorry, senhor."

Deirdre scanned the landscape. "Maybe there's another cave."

"Even if there is ... there's no telling where it would lead to," Ben said. "It looked to me like that cave we went through might be the only way in and out of here. Anyhow, we can't just sit here. Let's start looking along the cliffs."

As they continued walking, the rain gradually subsided. Stopping by the huge white cocoon-like column they had seen earlier, odd bumps and holes in the side of the cliff next to the giant cocoon caught Deirdre's attention. "Ben, look at this."

With his hand, he rubbed mud from the rock face. He stared, as if in a trance, at two indentations in the stone. "Dee, give me that bracelet ... the one the Chief gave you."

Deirdre dug into her pocket, pulled out the bracelet, and handed it to Ben.

"Miguel, Demetrio, com'ere," Ben shouted. "Whaddya make of this?"

They rushed to the cliff area where Ben stood with mud dripping from his hands. He pointed to the two odd holes in the stone. "Is it my imagination, or is one of those small holes in the side of the cliff shaped like a butterfly?"

Demetrio bent down, scooped up some water from a puddle, and splashed it onto the area of the indentations. As mud washed off the rock, the shape of the indentations became more apparent. He leaned toward the rock surface and squinted. "Looks like a butterfly to me. And this one next to it looks like three little worms or something."

"You mean they look like fossils?"

"How about three twisted prongs?" Deirdre added.

Ben then held up the Chief's bracelet from which the two gold charms dangled.

They all glanced at each other with eyes bulging.

"*No-no-nossa Senhora Aparecida*, the charms ... they look the same as those holes in the rock," Miguel stuttered.

Deirdre grabbed Ben's arm, and her mouth fell open. "Omigosh, the charm bracelet. The Chief said that I might need it. Remember? But what does this mean? Whadda we do now?"

Ben held the bracelet close to the stone surface. "It looks like these charms might fit right into those small holes in the stone." Hesitating at first, he pushed the butterfly charm into the corresponding indentation. The charm fell into place with a *click*.

Deirdre felt a fluttery feeling in her stomach. The others stood completely still with eyes darting from side to side.

Demetrio held the palms of his hands up in front of him. "So now what?"

At that moment, a sharp, tearing sound, like somebody ripping a bed sheet apart, screeched up the cliff with earsplitting intensity.

They all gazed up and stepped back.

The huge white, fuzzy cocoon-like column *rumbled*, *groaned*, *hissed*, and *squealed* before finally cracking and splitting open from top to bottom like a giant zipper. A white fluffy structure, the height of a five-story building, protruded from the giant cocoon sending a shower of snowflake-sized dander into the air. All at once, the column burst wide open, and shredded pieces of the cocoon-like structure fell to the ground like chunks of white, fuzzy plaster.

A colossal, white creature, at least fifty feet tall with six legs emerged. Two enormous appendages *snapped* outward from its body and unfolded with a thunderous *whap*, displaying two magnificent pure white wings like that of a butterfly, each spreading out fifty or more feet from the body. From the top of its head, two antennae whipped about like downed live power lines. A moment later, the enormous insect let out an ear-piercing *shriek*. It took a couple of steps forward, leaped into the air, and flew into the sky like a Boeing jumbo jet. The *whoosh* of the massive wings knocked everybody to the ground. The creature then disappeared over the mountain.

One by one, Miguel, Demetrio, Deirdre, and Ben staggered to their feet.

"Holy cow," Ben exclaimed. "You were right about the Amazon jungle, Dee. There *are* weird flying creatures here. I can't believe my eyes. Now I feel like I'm in Jurassic Park."

Deirdre turned to Ben and blew out a quick breath. "What was that thing?"

"There's no mistaking those wings. That, my dear … as far as I could tell, was a butterfly … a giant, white butterfly."

"How 'bout that?" Miguel said calmly. "We free a monster butterfly. It did not even help us. It just fly away. A lot of good that charm did us."

Deirdre nudged Ben with her elbow. "The other charm, try the other charm."

"What will that do? Make huge snakes come out of the rock?" Miguel said.

Ben leaned toward the cliff. "Well, here goes."

He inserted the second charm into the corresponding hole. The three twisted prongs of the charm *clicked* perfectly into place.

Deirdre bit her lip trying to imagine what would happen next.

Soon, a deafening *stretching* sound echoed through the garden. The ground shook and *rumbled* like a small earthquake.

Deirdre held on to Ben. Demetrio held on to Miguel.

The low-pitched stretching sound continued, sometimes *cracking* like a whip, sometimes *grinding* and *squealing*.

Miguel looked up at the cliff and across the meadow, but appeared puzzled as to where the noise came from. It echoed off the surrounding cliffs.

The shaking ground subsided, and they managed to stand up.

Demetrio turned toward the canyon and pointed. "I think it's coming from over there."

They scurried to the location where the root bridge formerly spanned the canyon. Standing at the edge, Deirdre found herself before a mammoth root-like structure growing out of the cliff, reaching out and intertwining like great, slithering snakes across the canyon.

As the roots grew and wound around each other, they *groaned* mournfully like a truck with bad brakes. Deirdre held her hands over her ears to muffle the deafening clamor and thuds as the thick root-like structures reached the other side of the canyon and pierced the earthen bank like giant spears.

Eventually, the collection of roots evolved into a make-shift bridge spanning the entire width of the canyon. With the bridge complete, the roots ceased moving.

For an instant, Miguel's breathing stopped.

Deirdre broke into a tentative smile that broadened.

Demetrio eased one foot onto the root structure. After standing for a moment, he started to walk across the newly-formed bridge. Once on the other side, he motioned to the others. "C'mon."

Ben took Deirdre's hand. All three started to cross the bridge. Halfway across, Miguel stopped and ran back toward the cliff area.

Deirdre turned and drew her eyebrows together. "Miguel, where are you going?"

He didn't answer. They waited.

Finally, Miguel ran to the bridge holding Deirdre's bracelet in his hand. "Senhora Deirdre, the bracelet. We left it in the cliff."

"Oh, thank you, Miguel. I'd better hold on to that."

They proceeded across the canyon and reached the entrance to the cave.

Pausing for a moment, Deirdre gazed back one last time at the magical land before entering the cave.

Chapter 33

Overcoming Fear

THE SPIRALING CHASM seemed to go easier and faster for Deirdre and the others on their journey back down the cave. So focused on reaching the bottom, they walked right by Derk's limp body lying in the deep crevice.

When they reached the lower region of the cave, Deirdre halted. "Oh, no. That tiny hole again."

One-by-one, they crawled down through the small opening onto a narrow ledge in the lowest area of the cave to find their only-known exit completely flooded. The passageway to the outside, now entirely submerged, made it difficult to tell if the outlet to the stream area still existed. They paced near the water's edge.

"*Nossa!*" Demetrio exclaimed. "That storm make river rise fast."

"I'll say," Ben said. "It must be the drainage basin for the entire area. I guess we'll have to just sit here and wait for the water to subside. There's no way I'm going in there."

"But that could be days, maybe weeks, or even months, senhor," Miguel added.

"What?"

"This is just beginning of rainy season. Much more rain will come. The river along mountain could get even higher and stay that way for very long time. We have to do something soon, senhor, or we could be trapped here until we starve to death."

The area where they stood, dark and barely wide enough for the four of them to stand, got smaller by the minute as the water continued to rise.

Deirdre stepped back, looked around, and started to tremble. "Everything is closing in around me. I gotta get outta here."

Ben held on to her.

"It is just a short way," Miguel said. "We can swim."

Ben rubbed the back of his neck and winced. "You mean underwater?"

"Just till we get out of the cave. Then we cross the river."

Deirdre gave a darting gaze at the cave walls and then at the water. "Ben, remember how your mother saved you from that pool. You lived because you weren't alone. You're not alone now. You can do it. We'll swim together. I hafta get outta here."

"Don't forget. It might not go down for weeks," Miguel said. "We have to take a chance. The longer we wait, the more it will close in on us and force us to go back up the cave. I think I know which way to swim under the surface to get to the cave exit and the river. Once we get there ... we just have to take our chances."

Miguel and Demetrio dove into the flooded passageway with a splash.

Treading water, Miguel waved his arm at Deirdre and Ben. "C'mon, you have no choice."

Deirdre and Ben glanced at each other, took deep breaths, grasped hands, and plunged into the churning torrent.

The four of them swam frantically underwater, bits of vegetation swirling all around them.

The current became increasingly swift as Deirdre and Ben struggled to catch up to Miguel and Demetrio in the debris-ridden channel.

Although a good swimmer, the driving current broke Deirdre's grip on Ben's hand. She thrashed around trying to feel for him in the murky water. *Oh, my God, where's Ben?* She briefly circled back, but couldn't find him. *Maybe he's ahead of me.* Struggling to hold her breath, she turned and continued swimming toward the exit.

* * *

Miguel and Demetrio emerged from the deep, muddy channel at the cave exit. The swelling river around them roared and slapped angrily against the car-sized boulder just beyond the cave. They reached out and clung on to a portion of it still above the water level. After catching their breaths, they pulled themselves onto the life-saving rock.

"Where are the others?" Miguel asked, breathing hard.

231

Demetrio coughed and rubbed his eyes. "They were right behind me."

Deirdre emerged gasping for breath. She looked up at Miguel and Demetrio on the boulder, swam toward them, but the current started to take her away. Demetrio jumped back in, grabbed her outstretched arm and pulled her toward the rock. He pushed her up onto the side of it. Miguel grabbed her arm and pulled her out of the river.

She panted and coughed, then turned her head toward the cave. "Where's Ben?" she shrieked. "Ben!"

* * *

Deep under the surface, Ben struggled and gurgled his way through the cave exit, flailing his arms and legs wildly. Floating upward, he raised his head and found a tiny air pocket against the ceiling of the cave exit tunnel. His nose almost touched the upper surface. He took a long, deep breath, hoping to suck in what little oxygen existed in the air pocket. As he rested, his mind raced, thinking the worst.

He felt something grab his leg and pull him back under. Garbled noises bubbled through the water, and Ben found himself wrestling with somebody in the depths of the dark, underground river.

* * *

On the boulder, Deirdre knelt and searched the water's edge. A head, gasping for air, burst out of the river with a frightening splash.

Deirdre sprang up and yelped. "Ben! It's Ben!"

Something or someone pushed him toward the rock. Right behind Ben a second head popped up, winded and struggling to breathe. Miguel and Demetrio reached out and pulled both men onto the rock.

As Ben lay by Deirdre's side coughing and breathing heavily, the other man, holding his bleeding side, collapsed and grimaced in pain.

While hugging Ben, Deirdre tilted her head and stared with narrow eyes at the dark-skinned stranger. "You're one of those men with Reverend James—"

Still catching his breath, Ben interrupted, "He saved my life. I would have never made it out of there without him. I didn't even know which way to go after a while."

Facing Deirdre, the man took a deep breath. "They left me for dead. My name is Derk. I worked for Reverend James. This whole trip turned out to be a lie. I meant no harm to you. Miss Gardner, please forgive me. I'm sorry he took your parrot."

Deirdre held Ben's head on her lap. Feeling confused, and not knowing whether to be angry or grateful, she glanced around as if looking for answers.

Miguel rose to his feet and peered across the river. "We can't stay here. I think we can make it across. Just let the current take you to that bend down the river. You should be able to grab on to something there. Let's try to stick together as much as we can."

They all nodded in agreement and slid into the river holding hands. The current took them downstream and toward the far-side bank. Miguel reached the bend first. He grabbed on to a small spindly tree leaning out of the bank. After dragging himself ashore, he took several deep breaths, waded back into the water, and pulled Deirdre, and then Ben, onto dry land. Panting to catch their breaths, the three sprawled on a grassy area at the water's edge.

Holding on to each other, Demetrio and Derk drifted a few yards farther downstream before reaching the bank. Demetrio put his arm around Derk, helped him out of the river, and both collapsed onto the grass next to the others.

Deirdre sat up and watched as Derk held his hand on his side. His face twisted in pain. "Miguel," she said, "we need to rest." She motioned her head toward Derk. "And before moving on, don't you think we should tend to this man's injury?"

Miguel and Demetrio examined the oozing knife wound in Derk's side. Demetrio took off his shirt, tore off a piece, folded it over the wound, and applied pressure. Derk jerked and moaned.

"Easy, amigo," Demetrio said.

Miguel then tied the rest of Demetrio's shirt around the injured man's torso and over the wound area. Derk moaned slightly again before settling back on the ground.

Miguel glanced around at his companions. Everybody appeared exhausted. "We'll take a break here for a while."

After resting for about thirty minutes, they got to their feet and headed back into the forest. With help from Demetrio and Ben, Derk kept up with the group. The sound of the rushing water faded as Ben stopped and glanced back at the mountain for a moment.

"What's the matter?" Deirdre asked. "C'mon."

"The white butterflies ... they're gone. I don't see a single one. And I wonder where that giant, white butterfly went."

Chapter 34

Help from the Sky

MAKING HIS WAY through an open field, Reverend James climbed over a small knoll. "Which way, Luis?"

"Straight," Luis said, pointing. "We must cross stream just ahead."

Filipe, who held on to Richard's pet carrier, hurried to catch up.

At the bottom of the hill, Reverend James glanced back and yelled to Filipe coming over the rise. "C'mon. You got the bird?"

"Do not worry, chefe. The bird is safe with me," Filipe shouted.

Just then, something *whizzed* through the air and, with a *thud*, stopped Filipe in mid-stride. He grimaced, fell to his knees, and dropped Richard's carrier, which rolled partially down the hill.

Reverend James whirled around and did a double-take.

Blood streamed down the front of Filipe's shirt, and the head of an arrow protruded from his chest. He fell, face-down, into the mud. The tail of an arrow jutted eerily upward from his back.

About thirty yards behind Filipe, stood a half dozen Indian men. One of them, with a bright red stripe clearly visible down the left side of his face, slowly lowered a bow to his side.

Luis took off in the direction of the stream.

Not wanting to contend with angry Indians apparently seeking revenge, thoughts of escape raced through the Reverend's mind. *But I can't lose this bird now!* Reaching down, he grabbed Richard's carrier and ran. Crashing through the vegetation, tree fronds slapped his body like whips.

The Indians took chase.

Reverend James made it to the small stream where he saw Luis standing on the other side. He splashed wildly through the water. When he reached Luis beyond the far bank, he stopped, glanced back, and noticed the Indians had halted at the edge of the stream.

As the Reverend motioned to start running again, Luis raised his arm and yelled, "Chefe, do not worry. They will not cross. This side of stream is forbidden land to the Indians. We should be safe now."

Reverend James stopped, looked back at the Indians, and sneered.

Then some of them raised their bows.

As several arrows arced through the air, Luis, wide-eyed, bolted into a grove of trees. The Reverend took cover. One arrow lodged into a tree in front of him. Others fell to the ground nearby.

Running, the Reverend made his way through scrubby bushes and grasses into another open field where he found Luis sitting on the ground breathing hard. Hoping he had put a safe distance between himself and the Indians' arrows, he sat down next to Luis.

The two men barely caught their breath when an ear-splitting *shriek* echoed across the sky. The Reverend looked up, eyes squinting against the sun. A massive bird-like creature, with white wings flapping gracefully, approached from above and headed directly toward them.

"What the—"

Luis looked up. "What's that? A giant bird?"

Reverend James froze and started to back up slowly. "My God ... what is that flying thing? It can't be a bird. No. Look at those wings and all those legs. I think it's a giant insect of some sort. I can't believe my eyes. It looks like a ... a giant butterfly!"

As the creature got closer, Luis ran wildly into the brush.

The Reverend started to run again, and the giant butterfly swooped down toward him. The wind of the flapping wings knocked him to the ground. He dropped Richard's carrier but managed to grab it. The butterfly circled around and went into another dive. Its legs knocked the Reverend to the ground once more, and his backpack flew through the air. He dropped Richard's carrier a second time, got to his feet, and ran into the forest canopy.

The butterfly swooped down one more time, and with two of its eagle-like claws, snatched Richard's carrier and the backpack off the ground.

Wiping his brow, Reverend James turned and looked warily up at the giant creature as it disappeared over the tree tops with the backpack and Richard's carrier in tow.

* * *

Out of breath and feeling dizzy, Reverend James eventually caught up to Luis and, together, they made their way to the bank of the Aripuana River. They located their canoe, still parked near the shore, and carried it to the water's edge. The Reverend climbed in. Luis pushed off, jumped in, and started paddling.

"Senhor, the rain ... it make the current strong. It should not take long to go down river."

Reverend James slumped in the front of the boat and cursed under his breath. "Damn." He glared at Luis. *Moron! He didn't help me. He just ran away like a frightened rabbit to save his own hide.*

Hardly speaking a word to Luis during the journey down the river, the Reverend gazed with an unfocused stare into the rainforest.

A couple hours later, Luis looked up and pointed to the encampment ahead. "Senhor James, soon we be back in the village. When will you pay me?"

The Reverend turned around, pulled a pistol from his pants, and pointed it at Luis. "Right now."

Luis stood, dropped the paddle, and trembled. The Reverend squeezed the trigger, and the gun fired. Luis fell backwards and splashed into the water. As his lifeless body drifted toward the far shore, two large caimans basking in the sun slithered into the water and cruised toward Luis's body.

The Reverend calmly picked up the paddle and continued rowing toward the encampment. With every stroke of the oar, he schemed and plotted. *They think they've won — that professor and his wife. Forget the bird. There's other ways to make money.* Reaching the shore, he yanked the boat out of the water and focused on his next move.

* * *

Farther back in the rainforest, Deirdre held on to Ben's arm as they made their way to a clearing. Miguel and Demetrio helped Derk, who continued to bleed slightly from his knife wound.

Chief Tobauqua and the Indian with the red stripe, along with several other Indians, stood at the far side of the clearing.

A deafening *shriek* echoed through the valley.

Ben jolted his head up. "Look, it's that giant butterfly we released from that huge cocoon in the magic garden."

The butterfly, with colossal wings flapping gracefully, approached the clearing. It held its wings out, went into a glide, descended slowly, and made a soft landing directly in front of Deirdre.

Deirdre threw her hand to her chest and shuffled back a couple of steps.

At first, the butterfly simply stared down at Deirdre with huge, grayish-blue, beach-ball-sized eyes. Its flowing eyelashes cast elongated shadows of black streaks across the ground. Then, one after another, two of its claws peeled open like flowers opening in time-lapsed photography. The backpack and Richard's carrier rolled gently out onto the ground at Deirdre's feet. The gold medallion Reverend James stole from the young Indian girl tumbled out of the backpack.

The butterfly, still looking down at Deirdre, cocked its head back and forth, slowly nodded, and softly blinked its enormous eyes as if trying to communicate with her.

Deirdre felt a sense of mystical euphoria and unusual warmth radiating through her body.

The Indians fell to their knees.

The butterfly then spread its wings and sprang off the ground in one giant leap. It flapped its wings, took off into the sky with a *whoosh*, and disappeared over the tree tops toward the distant mountain.

All, including the Indians, converged on Richard's carrier.

Deirdre picked it up. Feeling almost faint, she held it up to her watery eyes and peered inside. At first, unable to focus, she didn't see anything.

Then, from inside the carrier, came the familiar little voice. "Hi, Mommy. Are you okay?"

She briefly closed her eyes and pressed the palm of her hand to her heart. "Yes, Mommy is okay."

After letting Richard out of the carrier, she pulled him close to her face and smothered him with kisses. He pressed his beak to her lips and made a kissing sound. She then placed him safely back into his carrier.

Ben hugged Deirdre and gazed in at Richard. The Indians, Miguel, Demetrio, and even Derk gathered around Deirdre and Ben.

Miguel picked the medallion off the ground, showed it to Deirdre, and remarked, "Huh, once a thief, always a thief." He pulled the bracelet from his pocket and handed it and the medallion to Ben.

Ben then handed them to Chief Tobauqua. "I believe these belong to you, Chief."

Deirdre added, "The bracelet ... it saved our lives. Now we give it back to you. It belongs to your people. But, Chief, please allow little Tiko to keep my necklace."

The Chief handed the medallion to the Indian with the red stripe and said, "Give this back to your daughter." He then turned to Ben. "There were three" —he nodded toward the Indian father— "he killed one of them." The leader and one other crossed the stream where we dare not go."

Ben lowered his head. "So, he got away."

"The leader of those men ..." The Chief gazed toward the mountain. "He touched the tree of fire?"

"You mean that tree guarding the other tree?" Ben asked.

The Chief gave an easy nod.

"Yeah, but nothing happened," Ben said, raising his arms with palms facing upward. "I don't understand" —he pointed toward the mountain— "the tree of fire is back there in the magic garden, but the Reverend got away."

"His evil ways not yet over. He no escape the tree of fire," the Chief said in a firm, but calm voice.

Ben gave the Chief a blank stare, and Deirdre shrugged. Neither one pressed the Chief any further as to what he meant.

"Chief, how can we thank you?" Deirdre asked.

"You have. You free spirit of our great medicine man from past."

"We did?" Deirdre poked her tongue into her cheek. "How do you know? I mean … why do you think that? You weren't in the magic garden with us. You don't know what happened there!" She tilted her head to one side. "Or do you?"

A smug grin crept across the Chief's face. "Many things you cannot understand about our people, and many things I cannot explain."

Deirdre simply smiled and nodded.

Ben took a step closer. "Chief, I'm going to do all I can to make sure those loggers don't come across that stream. I promise."

A faint glimmer of hope and trust radiated from the Chief's eyes. "Thank you, my friend." He then turned and led the other Indians silently away.

Deirdre peered into Richard's carrier. "Richard, we're going home."

Richard responded, "Gotta go bye-bye."

Chapter 35

The Gift

IN RUMPLED CLOTHES and with sweat running down her face, Deirdre rushed through the front door of Judy and Justin's house carrying Richard in his travel carrier.

Ben came through the door behind Deirdre. "We got your phone message the minute we landed," he said to Justin, who held the door open. "Sorry it's so late, but our plane didn't get in 'til almost midnight. We got here as quickly as we could."

Assuming the worst, Deirdre pressed her clasped hands to her lips. "How is she?"

Justin simply hung his head and led them into Penny's bedroom where she lay, her sunken cheeks pale, eyes barely open, and her ragdoll lying idly by her side. An IV dangled next to the bed.

Judy sat bedside, rocking in place, holding the fragile little girl's hand. As Deirdre walked into the room, Judy stepped away from the bed and hugged her. "Oh, Dee, you got here just in time." She brought her hand up beside her mouth as if to hide her words and whispered, "The doctors say her systems are shutting down now, and there's nothing more they can do. I brought her home to be with us. I couldn't stand the thought of her being in a hospital hooked up to all that ... that stuff that won't do her any good anyway. The IV is to manage her pain."

A hospice nurse, shaking her head, approached Deirdre. "I'm so sorry. It'll be a miracle if she makes it through the night," she said in a low voice.

Deirdre glanced down at Richard's pet carrier. *Yes, a miracle.*

Justin left the room for a minute and came back carrying two folding chairs. He set them up near where Deirdre stood.

Deirdre set the pet carrier on a nightstand, knelt by the bed, put her arms around Judy, and peered down at Penny.

Penny's eyes opened slightly. "Aunt Dee," she murmured in a weak, barely audible voice.

With a tear running down her cheek, Deirdre gently cupped her hands around Penny's face. "Hi, sweetheart."

Judy started to cry. Justin put his arms around her.

Penny coughed, and her breathing became labored. "Mommy, don't cry."

Judy reached out and held her hand. "Okay, Mommy won't cry. I love you." *Please, God, ... oh, God, do something. Save her!*

Deirdre felt her stomach quiver. "Jude ... um ... I know this may seem strange, but I'd ...uh, like to try something."

"What? Try what?" Justin asked, pulling Judy nearer to him.

"May I bring Richard close to Penny?"

The nurse glanced around. "Richard?"

"Richard's my companion parrot. Penny always liked him. Maybe he can at least give her some comfort."

"It can't hurt, I guess," the nurse responded.

Judy glanced at Deirdre with vacant eyes and simply nodded. "Sure, if you think it will help. She means everything to me—" Her chin trembled. "If she leaves us, part of me will go with her," she said in a low voice.

Deirdre opened the door to the pet carrier, and Richard stepped up onto her hand. She gave him a soft kiss on his beak. At first, she hesitated, then inhaled deeply and placed Richard on Penny's shoulder. She took Judy's hand, squeezed it, and took several steps backward, gently pulling Judy back with her. She bit her lip while waiting for something to occur.

Penny slowly turned her head toward Richard, and a faint smile crossed her ashen face. "Oh, Richard," she whispered.

Richard stood tall, spread his wings slightly, and became unnaturally still.

Deirdre felt her stomach churn. A minute passed, but it seemed like an hour. *Nothing. Nothing's happening.* She sat down on one of the folding chairs, leaned forward and fixed her eyes on Penny and Richard. Several more minutes passed.

"What are you looking at?" Judy said. "Are you expecting something to happen?"

Not wanting to give Judy false hopes, she gritted her teeth struggling to respond. She turned and gazed out the bedroom window, where the full moon shone brightly. "I'm not exactly sure, but—" Just then, a white dove landed on the sill. An inner light went on in Deirdre's head and her spine tingled. She turned and looked Judy directly in the eye. "Yes, Jude, I *am* waiting for something to happen."

A moment later, Ben's eyes bulged, and he pointed at Richard. "D-D-Dee," he said in a shaky voice.

Deirdre sprang out of the chair and clutched her chest.

The patch of blue feathers on Richard's forehead began to take on a soft, eerie glow. He then tilted his head toward Penny. The glow gradually brightened into a brilliant radiance that sparkled across the room. Soon Richard's entire body emanated a dazzling, bluish-white light. The glow crept down into Penny and burst into a mass of turquoise-blue energy that shimmered between her and Richard. White star-like sparkles came from nowhere and merged into Penny. Spasms rippled up and down her body. She jerked back and forth as if some force had taken control of her. Then she reached out to Richard, closed her eyes, and appeared to fall into a state of peacefulness.

For a moment, everyone in the room froze. The sparkles and the glow slowly faded. As the glow from Penny and Richard completely subsided, the white dove flew off and disappeared into the night.

Justin flopped down into a chair and sighed before speaking. "What in the world?"

Penny moaned and turned her head to one side.

Judy and the nurse both rushed up to the side of the bed. The nurse let out a huge breath. "What was that?" she asked, looking all around. She checked Penny's pulse and pulled the blanket snugly around her. "She's still with us ... appears to be sleeping now."

Judy leaned over and kissed Penny on the cheek. Her hand trembled as she caressed her daughter. "I love you, my little one."

Deirdre reached for Richard. His feathers ruffled and his eyes half closed, he wobbled as he stepped up onto her hand.

She kissed him on the top of his head and placed him back into his carrier. "Richard acts like every ounce of energy has been drained from him," she said, flopping down into her chair. "Come to think of it, I feel the same."

Judy put her hand over her lips and gave Deirdre a blank look. She then lowered her hand and opened her mouth, but nothing came out.

"I'm not sure what happened," Deirdre said to Judy, "but I believe we've just seen something wonderful and magical. Time will tell. Don't ask. I'll explain later. I think we just have to wait and see."

Appearing overwhelmed by what they had just witnessed, everybody in the room seemed overcome by exhaustion. Justin lay down on the floor. Judy sat on a stool and rested her head on the bed next to Penny. Ben started to doze off in the other folding chair.

The nurse sat in a chair at the edge of the bed. "Get some sleep everybody. Don't worry, I'll stay up and keep an eye on Penny and let you know if there is any reason to wake you during the night."

* * *

Early next morning, as the sun peeked through the bedroom window and flickered in Deirdre's face, she heard Penny's voice calling.

"Mom? Dad?"

Deirdre opened her eyes and looked up to find Penny trying to sit up in bed and reaching for her rag doll.

"Take it easy, sweetie," the nurse said in a soothing voice as she wiped a cloth across Penny's forehead.

One by one, the others woke up and glanced around.

Judy lifted her head, jumped up, and grabbed Penny's hand.

The nurse smiled at Judy. "I've never seen anything like it," she said, shaking her head. "It's remarkable. Ever since your sister put that bird on Penny's shoulder, her color started to come back, her eyes now look brighter, and her pulse is stronger. I don't understand."

Penny turned her head, and her eyes widened. "Mom!"

Glassy-eyed, Judy broke into a wide grin and hugged Penny. She gazed upward, almost screaming, "Oh, my God! You're better!" Her knees buckled, and she started to faint.

Justin caught and cradled her. "Judy, I can't believe it ... our baby is okay?" His eyes looked toward the heavens, and, for the first time in countless years, he thanked an unseen power.

Together, Justin and Judy laughed and cried at the same time.

Feeling her eyes get watery, Deirdre pressed her lips together and felt them spread into a smile.

Ben wrapped his arm around her.

From inside his pet carrier, Richard whistled.

Chapter 36

One Month Later

WITH THE TOP down, Deirdre at the wheel, and Judy in the passenger seat, the convertible raced down Route 209. Deirdre glanced over at Judy and yelled over the howling wind, "So you're still having trouble believing everything that happened on our trip to Brazil, huh?"

"Well ... *yeah*!" Judy yelled back. "It is kinda hard to believe. Incredible! And Richard is okay?" She leaned over and took a glimpse at the speedometer. "Hey, maybe you'd better slow down a bit, lead foot. There's traffic ahead."

Deirdre rolled her eyes at Judy as she slowed up. "Oh, yes, the vet said he seems just fine. Of course, I didn't tell him *everything*, if you know what I mean. He would have thought I was looney." She stopped behind traffic at a red light. "As you know, that's why Ben and I don't talk about it to *anyone*. Can you imagine what they would think of Ben at the college? I simply told the vet I thought a checkup for Richard would be a good idea since he was with us on our trip to Brazil."

"That makes sense."

"Oh, and guess what? Ya know that recurring dream I had ever since Penny got sick?"

"Yeah?"

"Don't have it anymore. Weird, huh?"

"I guess it's obvious now why you were having that dream in the first place. Hey, what ever happened with that book deal you were working on?"

"I have an appointment to meet with the publisher in New York. And Ben is going with me. We have a wonderful trip planned."

"Don't take this wrong, but I hope that trip won't be quite as adventurous as your last one."

"This ordeal with Richard and Penny ... it did make me realize that my writing is certainly not the most important thing in my life." She shrugged. "Say, I'll bet Penny's doctors are amazed, aren't they?"

"They can't find any sign of the cancer—truly a miracle. I don't know how I can ever thank you and Richard. Boy, you must've been really worried when Richard disappeared in the jungle. And that was before you even got to that magic garden."

"Instinct, I suppose. Probably just enchanted with the rainforest." She giggled. "Or maybe he spotted a pretty little female Blue-fronted Amazon."

When traffic started moving again, the car in front of Deirdre didn't go right away.

She laid on the horn and yelled, "C'mon, bud, get moving."

This time Judy rolled *her* eyes.

As Deirdre slowed up, rounded a curve and approached the driveway, Judy asked, "And what about Reverend James?"

"That's a good question. I presume he made his way back to the States. Julia stopped going to his church, and last I talked to her, which was very briefly, she didn't know. Since getting back home, Ben and I have been so busy getting resettled that we're just now starting to get back to normal. I'll ask her again tonight to see if she heard anything. You can bet he isn't home free after what he tried to do."

After Deirdre parked the car, Judy climbed out and grabbed a shopping bag from the back seat.

A vibrant and healthy-looking Penny ran out the front door of the house and onto the porch. A wide grin spread across her face. "Hi, Aunt Dee."

Deirdre walked up to the porch and hugged her.

"Look, my hair is starting to grow back," Penny said, patting the top of her head. "It feels so funny."

"You look wonderful, sweetie." At that moment, Deirdre reflected on the amazing journey that had brought them to this point.

"She's doing really well," Judy said.

"And she's so smart," Deirdre added. "Just think, she'll be able to do all the things she ever wanted to do. And, I just know she'll make a wonderful doctor someday."

"Wouldn't that be great!" Judy motioned her head toward the door. "Ya wanna come in for a drink? I've got some tea and soda. Or how 'bout a glass of wine?"

Deirdre looked at her watch. "Geez, I'd love to, but don't forget, we're going over to Oakwood Acres to visit Julia this evening after dinner. You, Justin, and Penny are still going, aren't you? Julia's gonna be amazed when she sees Penny. And we're taking Richard. The folks there just adore him, and it's been quite a while since they last saw him."

"Oh, yeah, that's right. We're going. And, by the way, thanks for taking me shopping."

Deirdre started to walk back to her car. "Okay, see ya later."

Judy put her hand up. "Oh, Dee, wait. Before you go … I've been meaning to ask you. What do you suppose that little Indian boy you told me about is doing right now? You know … the one you gave your necklace to."

"Tiko? Oh, I suppose he's running through the rainforest with the animals. He did have some sort of special relationship with the animals there."

* * *

At that same moment in the Brazilian rainforest, Tiko raced down a trail and stopped in front of the tall kapok tree with the hollow that now became familiar to him. Exploring his senses, he looked up. *I need to check on the little papagaio.* Deirdre's necklace dangled from his neck as he climbed the tree, leaned forward, and peered into the cavity.

Inside, a baby parrot, looking like nothing more than a tiny fuzzball, lay in a nest of wood shavings. As if too heavy for its body, the baby's head, topped with a few wisps of turquoise-blue feathers, wobbled as it rose up and appeared to look back at Tiko with wide eyes. A proud-looking adult Blue-fronted Amazon parrot sat on a nearby tree branch appearing unconcerned about the snooping boy.

Tiko squinted to get a better look into the nest. "What a beautiful baby papagaio you are. You grow bigger every day. Soon we will know each other better, my friend."

For a moment, Tiko closed his eyes. A sense of generations of Cinta Largos filled his thoughts, and mystical enchantment rushed through his body. He then shimmied back down the tree and darted away.

Chapter 37

Night Visitors

POUNDING HIS FIST on the desk, Reverend James rose from his chair, tipping it over and banging it against the wall. "Whaddya mean we have to close the home?"

Marlena stomped across the floor. "We haven't had a single new resident in months. In the meantime, Oakwood is doing great. They even have a waiting list of people wanting to get in. We can't pay the bills anymore. And since that trip to Brazil was a waste of time, I guess you'll just have to keep staging that phony healing act of yours." She crossed her arms. "Where is Derk anyway? I haven't seen him since you got back."

Wiping his brow with his handkerchief, he snapped back, "Had an accident in Brazil."

"An accident? What kind of accident? Is he okay?"

"Slipped off a cliff. I reached out and tried to save him, but—"

She stared at him with wide eyes. "But what? What?"

"Let me put it this way," he said with a heavy sigh. "I don't think we'll be seeing him anymore."

She put her hand over her mouth, then slid it down to her chest. "No! Are you kidding me? I can't believe this. Does Alicia know? Or does she think the two of you are still in Brazil?"

"Don't worry. I'll deal with her."

Marlena put her hands on her hips. "How? Like you deal with the residents that can't pay?"

Veins in the Reverend's neck protruded like vines creeping up a stone wall. He slapped his arm across the desk, scattering papers over the room. "What are you talking about?" he shouted.

"I think you know darn well what I'm talking about."

He stomped up to her and backhanded her across the face.

She fell to the floor, wiped a drop of blood from her lip, and scowled at him.

As he walked toward the office door, he turned to her and shouted, "What we need to do is eliminate our competition. Then we'll have the only senior living home in town!"

She wrinkled her forehead as she wiped more blood from her lip. "What's that supposed to mean? Wilcox already told you he doesn't want to sell Oakwood."

Reverend James simply sneered. "You're too stupid to understand." He stormed out of the room and slammed the door.

* * *

Later that evening across town in the community room at Oakwood Acres, Deirdre took Richard out of his carrier and set him on a portable perch as Ben and Julia watched and chatted. A dozen residents entered the room and started gathering around Richard. Soon, Judy, Justin, and Penny walked into the room from the main vestibule. Penny let go of their hands and dashed toward Julia.

Sitting on the sofa, Julia held out her arms. "I can't believe my eyes. Querida, come and give me a hug." Her face glowed as she embraced Penny. "You look so healthy and full of joy again. I am so happy for you."

"It's all because of Aunt Dee and Richard," Penny said in a bubbly voice.

Her eyes, sparkling with wonder, Julia turned to Deirdre. "You find a cure, Miss Dee? In the jungle? Did you find the special papagaio and the gift of healing?"

Deirdre looked over at Richard. "I did, Julia. As a matter of fact, I found a very special papagaio." Her voice cracked with emotion.

Throughout the evening, Richard entertained everyone by singing and talking. All laughed and took turns talking to Richard. Penny giggled, nonstop.

After a while, the room quieted down, and some of the residents started yawning.

Ben looked down at his watch and nodded to Deirdre, "Wow, it's going on nine already. I suppose we should get going and let these good people go to bed."

As her family headed toward the front door, Deirdre stayed sitting on the sofa. "Julia, I have an idea. How 'bout if Richard and I spend the night with you? He can entertain the residents at breakfast, and you and I can spend some time together tomorrow and catch up on things." She looked up at Ben. "Okay with you?"

"I suppose Cody and I can manage to have breakfast on our own tomorrow. Sure. You need some girl-time with Julia."

"Oh, Miss Dee, that would be so nice, but you and Richard should go home with Mr. Ben."

"You heard Ben. He doesn't mind. It'll be fun. I often let Richard sleep out of his cage. He sleeps just fine on this perch with the little tray underneath to catch his droppings."

"Okay, then I guess we better hit the sack as they say," Julia murmured.

After entering Julia's room, Deirdre set Richard's perch on a small table and flopped into Julia's recliner. "This will do me just fine."

"Miss Dee, don't worry if you hear me get up during the night. I sometimes go to the kitchen for a snack. I hope I won't wake up Richard."

"You won't bother us. Both Richard and I sleep like logs." She pulled a paperback book from her purse. "Maybe I'll read for a short while 'til I get sleepy. By the way, did you ever hear anything about Reverend James being back in town?"

"Yes. I heard he is back" —she yawned— "and preaching at his church as usual." Her eyes slowly closed.

Deirdre looked over at Richard, who nestled his head on his back and tucked one leg up against his breast, his typical sleeping position. "Good night, precious," she whispered.

As Julia turned in her sleep, Deirdre tipped her head back and fell asleep with an open book resting on her lap.

* * *

In the dead of night, a thin metal tool forced its way across the latch of the window in the community room. With a *click*, the window creaked open. The shadowy figure of a man, carrying a flashlight and a small sack, crawled through the open window and into the room.

Dim, recessed ceiling lights shined down on the unlit gas fireplace on the far wall. An occasional snore echoed from the bedrooms down the hall.

The man looked around, reached into the sack, and pulled out a small timing device wired to a spark igniter and a battery wrapped together with duct tape. After setting the timer, he placed it on a table by the fireplace.

He knelt down and pulled a white handkerchief and a wrench from his pocket. Leaning into the fireplace opening, he firmly fixed the wrench around the nut on the gas supply line along one side of the fireplace wall and turned it to loosen the connection. The gas started to *hiss* from the fireplace insert. He covered his nose with the handkerchief. The escaping gas *hissed* louder as he loosened the nut further on the connection.

* * *

Down the hall in her room, Julia awakened as her clock clicked 3:05 a.m. She crawled out of bed, grabbed a cup from her nightstand, and shuffled out the bedroom door into the hallway. The floor creaked as she entered the community room. With eyes squinting, she saw a figure kneeling by the fireplace.

The intruder whirled around, stood up, and his handkerchief fell to the floor. The light briefly hit his face.

Julia stopped midstride and stared for a moment at the man, who wore a black shirt, cargo pants, and gloves. She clutched at her chest, put her hand to her mouth, and gasped. "Rev—"

The furtive figure leapt forward and whacked the wrench across her head with a *thud*. She moaned and fell to the floor.

He glanced around, slipped the wrench back into his pocket, and crawled back out the open window. As he pulled the window pane shut, he took one last look into the room. The gas hissed loudly from the fireplace. On the table, the timing device ticked away.

* * *

In Julia's bedroom, Richard opened his eyes, lifted his head, and sensed something. He fluttered off his perch and out of the bedroom.

He flew down the hall into the community room and glided to the floor near where Julia lay groaning. Attracted by the hissing sound, he waddled in his typical pigeon-toed fashion toward the fireplace.

Julia lifted her head slightly, reached out and moaned, but then fell silent. Blood streamed down the side of her head.

Richard peered curiously at the nut on the hissing gas line. He shook his head rapidly back and forth in response to the odor and fell backwards for a moment. He then stepped forward, briefly hesitated as if thinking, and cocked his head. Seeing the nut, he couldn't resist the urge to turn it like he often did with the one on his food bowl attached to his play gym—a game to him.

He leaned forward, grabbed the nut with his beak and started to rotate it. Using his beak like a wrench, he let go of the nut repeatedly after each partial turn to readjust his grip. After a few turns, he stumbled. The hissing slowed. He reached for the nut again and continued twisting it. Fragments of his beak splintered and fell to the floor as he struggled to turn the nut. Eventually, the nut tightened, and he couldn't turn it any further. The hissing stopped.

Julia lifted her head and started to push herself up, but crumpled back down to the floor.

The room became quiet.

Chapter 38

The Aftermath

SUNLIGHT STREAKED through the window of Julia's bedroom. Deirdre stirred and looked around to find Julia's bed empty. Rubbing her eyes, she glanced over at Richard's perch. He wasn't there. Her stomach churned. She lunged out of the recliner, sending the still-open book from her lap flying across the floor.

"Julia? Richard?" Deirdre called out softly. Hearing no response, her voice turned more urgent. "Julia? Richard?" Her head jerked as a scream resonated down the hall. She grabbed her purse and dashed out of the bedroom into the community room.

There, a female attendant knelt next to Julia, who lay sprawled on the floor looking dazed and disoriented. Blood trickled from a gash on the side of Julia's head.

Deirdre trembled as she stooped and gently touched Julia's hand. "Oh, my God, Julia, are you okay?"

Mr. Wilcox arrived in the room at the same moment and wrinkled his nose. "Geez, I smell gas." He ran to the window, threw it open, looked around, reached down, and picked a handkerchief off the floor. As the attendant rose to her feet, he faced her and shouted, "Call 911. Get an ambulance. Hurry."

While the attendant reached for her cell phone, Mr. Bowdine and other Oakwood residents crept into the room with bewildered looks on their faces and converged around Julia. Deirdre and Mr. Wilcox helped Julia to a nearby sofa.

With a frantic gaze that flitted around the room, Deirdre pulled out her cell phone and pressed buttons. "Ben, something awful happened to Julia, and I don't know where Richard is. Get over here, now."

While lowering the cell phone from her ear, she called out with an emotion-choked voice, "Richard? Has anyone seen Richard?"

Several people shook their heads.

Soon an ambulance pulled up outside. Ben's car pulled up minutes later.

As a male medical technician tended to Julia, Ben rushed in. "I got here as soon as I could. What's going on?"

Deirdre, sitting next to Julia, looked up. "We're not sure. It looks like Julia fell or something. And I can't find Richard." She turned to the technician. "Can you tell what happened to her? Did she fall?"

"Maybe. I'm not sure. Looks like she got a nasty bump and a gash on the head, but I think she'll be okay. She'll need x-rays to be sure."

"Julia, what happened?" Deirdre asked.

"I was just going to the kitchen for a snack," she replied weakly, "like I always do. I see a man. I can't believe it. It looked like Reverend James. He was doing something at the fireplace."

Mr. Wilcox leaned toward Julia and raised his eyebrows. "The fireplace?"

He and Ben walked in that direction.

Julia went on, "I heard a hissing noise and smelled gas. Then he came at me and hit me with something. The next thing I know, I saw Richard" —she pointed— "over there, by the fireplace. Then I sort of blacked out."

Deirdre spun her head toward the fireplace where Ben, now crouched, wiped his forehead while gazing downward. Her face turned white with panic. "Richard? Did anybody see Richard? Where is he?"

She ran to the fireplace. Ben tried to stop her, but she pushed him aside. Looking down, her knees buckled, and she collapsed to the floor. A sudden coldness hit at the core of her heart. Disoriented at first, her muscles tightened, and she took quick short breaths. Her vision blurred as her eyes turned into watery globes. Then with her head drawing back stiffly, she let out a gut-wrenching scream. Once the first tear trickled down her cheek, the rest soon followed in an uncontrollable torrent.

"Nooo," she shouted. "Nooo!"

Shaking all over, she cupped her hands around Richard's lifeless body. Her chest heaved as tears streamed down her face. Unable to speak, she rose to her feet cradling her beloved Richard in her hands. With thoughts of denial racing through her head, and unable to accept what might be, she lifted Richard up to her face and attempted to give him mouth-to-mouth.

Ben put his hand on her shoulder. "Dee, Dee."

She lowered Richard's body away from her shaking head. "Richard, don't leave me!" She started to raise his limp body toward her face again.

Ben put his hand on her arm. "Dee ... stop."

She slowly turned her head toward Ben.

Ben's voice choked. "He's gone."

"No!" she said, raising her voice and vigorously shaking her head. "He can't be. Not my Richard!"

Ben put his arms around her and lowered his head. "I'm sorry, sweetheart. I'm so sorry."

All eyes on Deirdre, a numbing silence permeated the entire room.

One by one, everybody stepped aside, making a pathway for her as she turned and walked slowly, zombie-like with a blank stare, holding Richard close to her chest, toward the sofa where Julia sat.

The usually colorful Mr. Bowdine lowered his head and appeared to fight back tears. Deirdre sat down next to Julia, rocked uncontrollably back and forth, raised Richard to her face, and kissed him on the head.

* * *

Unable to fight back his own tears, Ben knelt down in front of Deirdre and lowered his head onto her lap and sobbed. He got up and sat on the sofa, put his arms around her, kissed her tear-soaked cheek, and petted Richard. Jagged black lines tracked down Deirdre's cheeks as her tears merged with day-old eyeliner and mascara. He squeezed her tightly, and together, they rocked back and forth as if trying to shake off their grief.

For the moment, Ben didn't say anything else to Deirdre, fearing that it was best to leave her alone.

A few minutes later, Ben got up, glanced at the small table and picked up the timing device. After examining it, he showed it to Mr. Wilcox. Together, they bent down by the fireplace and took a close look at the gas line connection.

Mr. Wilcox scratched his temple. "I don't understand. The gas line looks fine. Where did the gas come from? And why did we find Richard here?"

Ben knelt down and inspected the shiny wrench marks on the gas supply line connection nut. He picked up fragments of Richard's beak from the floor, rubbed them between his thumb and forefinger, and glanced back at Deirdre. His mind churned.

"What are you thinking?" Mr. Wilcox asked.

"I believe the intruder caused the gas to leak by loosening the gas line connection. Richard must've smelled the gas and flown to it."

"So, then how did the gas stop leaking?"

"You won't believe me when I tell you what I think. At home, Richard uses his beak to turn the nut on his food bowl. It's like a little game for him. He will keep turning the nut until it falls to the floor."

"Wait a minute," Mr. Wilcox said. "So, what you're saying is—"

"What I'm saying is, I believe, for whatever reason, Richard was apparently attracted to the fireplace by the hissing gas sound, spotted the nut, grabbed hold of it with his beak and turned it until he couldn't turn it anymore."

"You mean—"

Ben leaned forward. "That's right. Whether he actually knew what he was doing or not, he shut off the gas. And, in the process, was overcome by it."

"And that device?" Mr. Wilcox asked.

"A timing device. Looking at it, I'd say it was set to emit a spark that would ignite the gas. Apparently, it was set to allow enough time for the gas to build up in the room while also giving the intruder time to get away. But Richard apparently shut off the leaking gas before too much escaped."

Mr. Wilcox held the handkerchief in front of Ben and pointed to the initials, JJ. He brought his hand up beside his mouth and leaned toward Ben's ear. "I believe Julia is right. Apparently Reverend James is desperate to eliminate his competition."

Ben's mouth fell open, and he jerked his head back.

Julia looked up with dazed eyes. "I thought it looked like Reverend James. What day is it?"

"Thursday," Mr. Wilcox replied. "Why?"

"On Sunday, he will have his service, but I hear many followers are angry for some reason, even his own wife."

"You know I have to call the police. Of course, there will be an investigation. And I'll tell them who we think the intruder is, but I'm sure, at first, all they can do is question him."

"That's okay," Ben said with a steady voice. "Maybe it's about time we went to one of his services."

Deirdre gave Ben a blank stare as she lifted Richard's lifeless body to her face and caressed him.

Chapter 39

A Solemn Occasion and a Showdown

GULPING COFFEE the following morning, Reverend James stumbled over his words as he talked on the phone. "I don't know why you'd want to talk to me, but ... okay." As he hung up the phone, he scraped a hand through his hair.

Marlena walked into the room. "What's with you this morning? Who was that on the phone?"

"Oh, just one of our followers going through some hard times. I offered to go over to his house and talk. I'll probably be gone a couple of hours."

He put his hands over his sweating face, then stood up and reached in a pocket for his handkerchief, but came up empty. His muscles twitched and his stomach quivered. After staring into space for a moment, he stomped out the door, got into his car, and drove off.

Cruising by Oakwood Acres, he slowed down, pounded his hand on the steering wheel and sped away.

* * *

Fifteen minutes later, Reverend James arrived at the East Stroudsburg Police Station. As soon as he entered, two men in dress shirts and ties greeted him.

"Reverend James?" one of them said.

"Yes," he said, faking a smile.

"I'm Detective Lee Redd. This is my partner, Detective Phil Walker."

"So, what's this all about?"

"If you don't mind, Reverend, we'd like to ask you a few questions. This way please."

Detective Redd led him to an interrogation room.

After two hours of questioning, they escorted the Reverend to the front door of the station. Detective Redd said, "For now, don't plan on taking any vacations, Reverend. We'll be back in touch."

Detective Walker scowled at the Reverend. "Yeah, you better believe you'll be hearing from us again … real soon."

* * *

On Saturday, with somber faces, Deirdre and Ben, followed by Judy, Justin, and Penny, walked under a tall metal trellis with a sign overhead that read, Forever Pet Cemetery. A crowd of others, including Julia, Dean Haase and Ada, Woody and Sylvia, Mr. Wilcox, and dozens of Oakwood residents, shuffled into the cemetery.

Clutching a tiny wooden casket in the palm of her hands in front of her chest, Deirdre led the way to the gravesite. As she placed the casket on the ground near Richard's ready grave, a strong, eerie breeze interrupted the calm air and rustled through a nearby oak tree. A white dove perched majestically on one of its branches.

Deirdre knelt down and slowly lowered the casket into the burial place. She scooped up a handful of dirt from a nearby pile, held it over the open grave, and slowly allowed it to dribble through her fingers onto the tiny casket.

Penny left Judy's side, scooped up a handful of dirt, and gently trickled it into the grave. "Thank you for giving me back my life, Richard. I will miss you so much."

With lips pressed together, Judy took Penny's hand and looked at her with wet, dull eyes.

Sniffling, and wiping tears off her cheeks with her hand, Deirdre stood and peered up at the oak tree. Her lips quivered and her voice cracked as she spoke. "Richard, you're a hero. I believe you were put on this earth for a purpose. You saved Penny's life. Then you sacrificed your own life to save many others." Her knees buckled, and she slumped to the ground as tears streamed down her face. With a lump in her throat, she tilted her head toward the sky and went on. "Goodbye, my dear, Richard. I promised I would take care of you forever. I don't know how, but I still vow to keep that promise."

Ben helped Deirdre to her feet. After standing still with bowed heads for a while, everybody walked slowly away from the gravesite without saying a word.

As Ben drove out of the cemetery, Deirdre dabbed her eyes with a tissue.

* * *

On Sunday, Reverend James prepared for his morning service in the Salvation Temple office.

Stephen walked in lugging a large can. "The urns are filled with oil. Everything is ready."

"Good," said the Reverend. "Where's your mother?"

"I didn't see her this morning."

After giving a wandering gaze, the Reverend hurried out of the office and to the side of the pulpit where he watched as people filed into the church and took seats.

Michael and Lily walked in holding hands. Michael had an uncharacteristically angry look on his face. Others appeared stoic.

A man wearing a hoodie and black shoes entered the church and took a seat in the back row.

After checking his watch, Reverend James strolled out to the pulpit. Flames shot out of the two huge vessels behind him as he started to speak. "Is there a God? Yes, but you make your own destiny. There will be no future if we don't help each other. I am your gatherer. I will care for your money and possessions so that you don't squander it away. When you are sick, I will heal you. If you are old, I will shelter you and—"

The squeak and loud bang of a door opening and closing to the side of the pulpit interrupted the sermon. Marlena and Sheila emerged, followed by Deirdre and Ben. Reverend James' sermon disintegrated into a stutter.

"And what? Murder them?" Marlena shouted.

Holding up a syringe and bottle, Sheila faced the congregation of a few dozen people and shouted, "If your beloved mother, father, or friends could no longer pay to stay in the Church's Senior Living Center, this is what your Reverend used on them … to murder them."

Lily stood up from her seat crying and yelled, "He's not a healer. He's a monster. That explains why my mother died so suddenly. We fell behind on our payments. He did it. He killed my mother!"

Congregation members began to chatter. Even the Reverend's most faithful employee, Joan, did not stay quiet any longer. She stood up from her usual spot in the front row and announced, "Remember that elderly lady he claimed to have healed of her cancer not very long ago? You wanna know why you haven't seen her in church since then? She died. That's why."

A hush came over the congregation.

Sheila faced the Reverend and shouted directly at him. "Not only are you a phony healer, you're not even a real minister." She turned to his wife. "Isn't that right, Marlena?"

The congregation quieted. Marlena's expression dulled, and she lowered her head, hiding her face with her hair. Then, apparently crumpling under scrutiny, she raised her head, and with hesitation in her voice, spoke up. "It's true."

One of the newer female church followers then chimed in. "My husband and I were suspicious of how things were run here. So, while he was away in Brazil, we checked into the church finances. Everything he took from all you people is gone. He used it for himself."

The mysterious man with the hoodie and black shoes stood up in back of the church and slowly strode up the center aisle. All eyes turned to him, and everybody quieted down as he clicked his way toward the pulpit and lowered the hood from his head.

Reverend James trembled with disbelief as he stared at the man. "You! Y-You're dead!"

Derk looked around and announced to the congregation, "He left me for dead in the rainforest. He also left Professor Gardner and his wife, Deirdre, to die there. But we all survived to reveal the truth about him. I'm ashamed I ever believed in him and that I worked for this disgraceful, self-proclaimed man of the cloth."

Teary-eyed and baring her teeth, Deirdre stomped forward. "And he tried to burn down Oakwood Acres, but failed. I lost my beloved parrot, who gave his life and saved the home and everybody inside."

The angst-ridden congregation turned into a mutinous mob and gradually started to move menacingly down the aisles in the direction of the pulpit.

After glancing at Derk, Deirdre, and Marlena, the Reverend glared defiantly at the congregation as they, staring with cold, hard eyes, walked toward him. He jerked to the side, but some of the people blocked his path. "Brothers and sisters, do not listen to them. What they say is not true. You know me. I have healed you. I have loved you as my own children."

"You are a disgrace," one follower said, jerking away to avoid contact. "The only person you have ever loved is you."

Reverend James held his hands up, palms toward the angry mob closing in on him. *How dare they? They never deserved a man of my caliber.* His arrogance quickly turned to panic. He shuffled backward and felt weakness in his legs as the angry mob crept closer and closer. "P-P-Please. Listen to-to me," he begged. "Lies, it's all lies."

He stumbled into one of the flaming vessels. The vessel overturned and crashed to the floor, and he slipped into the flaming oil. His screams filled the church as the flames, as well as shame, engulfed him like the mouth of a huge, fiery snake grabbing hold of its prey.

* * *

Deirdre and the others watched in horror as the raging fire surrounded the Reverend. The flames above his head took on the shape of the Devil himself. Everybody backed away as a black hole opened up in the stage. More flames reached out of the hole, like grisly, fiery arms, and pulled him downward. He squealed as the devilish arms tore his body apart into two forms. One form fell to the floor, burning. The other, more ghostly, continued to scream, clawing at the edge of the hole as something or some force pulled it downward. Then with one rapid motion, the Reverend's ghostly figure vanished, sucked into the black hole. The Devil's face above the flames disappeared.

As the black hole closed, the physical body of Reverend James smoldered on the stage. The fire raged on, and the flames leaped, engulfing the curtains and furniture. Soon the whirling inferno crept up the walls, crackling, with black smoke spiraling outward. Everybody screamed and ran out of the church.

Outside, as the blare of arriving firetruck sirens filled the air, the churchgoers watched as the old clapboard church burned and started to crash to the ground.

Ben squinted and turned to Deirdre. "I remember what Chief Tobauqua said about that tree of fire. He said, 'he who is evil will find fire.' Reverend James did touch that tree."

Deirdre looked up at Ben, clenched her lips, and clung to him as the church smoldered into ashes. "He found the fire, and Satan found his soul. He got what he deserved."

Chapter 40

Six Years Later

A LIGHT SNOW fell outside the window of Judy's house. Deirdre sat at the kitchen table with Judy, both sipping hot tea. Deirdre's cell phone lay on the table.

A now fourteen-year old Penny, wearing a short, black dress, a fleece jacket flung over her arm, entered the kitchen, approached her aunt, and hugged her. "I'm so happy to see you, Aunt Dee. If I had known you were coming over tonight, I wouldn't have made plans."

Deirdre smiled as she brushed a strand of long blond hair from Penny's face. "Now, don't you worry. We'll spend some time together soon. By the way, young lady, I hear you're doing terrific in school. Look at you. Not only are you going to make a great doctor, you're going to be a beautiful one. Bet you'll send those boys into a tailspin tonight."

Penny blushed. "Oh, Aunt Dee, you always make me feel so special."

"You are special ... and so dear to all of us."

A horn beeped outside.

"Oh, that's my friend Brittany. Her mom is driving us to the school dance. Gotta run, Mom. Don't worry 'bout me. I'll be home on time."

"But the weather scares me. Make sure Brittany's mom is aware we're supposed to get some snow and ice tonight. It looks like it's starting to snow now. Got your cell phone?"

"Yup, got it."

"Have fun and please be careful."

"We will, Mom. Don't worry."

Penny gave each a hug and dashed out the front door leaving Deirdre and Judy to chat among themselves.

"So, how's that children's book of yours doing since it was published?" Judy asked. "Penny and I thought it was a great read."

"Not bad. Sales are starting to pick up. Of course, I'm really excited about the book I just finished. You know, the one about Richard. I hope to hear from the publisher any day now."

"Wow, that *is* exciting. Anything new as a result of Ben's report?"

"Oh, yeah. I'm really proud of him. It took a few years, but his report to the commission finally resulted in a temporary halt to logging in that stream area in Brazil I told you about."

"That's wonderful."

"Yeah, but I still worry about the Indians there. Julia got a letter from her brother, Miguel. He said Doctor Ryman died. Who'll take care of the children in that village?" Deirdre became teary-eyed.

"Dee, you can't save the world. That's not your problem."

"It's not only that. Thinking about everything that happened back then ... I can't get over losing Richard. You know how I loved him. He was so special."

"Special? Penny wouldn't be here today if it weren't for Richard. Neither would all those people at Oakwood." Judy reached for Deirdre's hand. "What a hero he was. Maybe that was his purpose in life. And he did have a wonderful life with you."

"He did, but I miss him so much."

"Wherever he is now, I'll bet he misses you too."

While Judy got up to pour more tea, Deirdre's cell phone rang. She answered.

"Yeah, I'm still at Jude's, and I'm leaving to come home in a couple minutes, sweetheart. Okay, don't worry, I'll be careful."

She hung up and slid the phone into her purse.

"That was Ben. It's late. I better get home before the weather gets too bad."

Judy looked out the window. "Are you sure you wanna go? It looks pretty nasty out there already. You can certainly stay here for the night."

Deirdre gathered up her purse and coat and walked to the door. "Oh, I'll be fine. Talk to you tomorrow. See ya."

Jude held the door open. "Drive carefully."

* * *

Deirdre shivered as she inserted the key into the car door. "Brrr, this weather is just too much for me anymore. Gotta look in to someplace warmer," she mumbled as she settled herself into the seat and turned the key. The engine turned, but didn't start. "Oh, no. Come on, little car. We've been together a long time. Don't die on me now." She turned the key again. The motor started with a *vroom*.

She backed out of the driveway, turned on the lights, wipers, and radio, and headed down the road toward home. After a while, she started mouthing the words along with a song on the radio, Rod Stewart's, "Tonight's the Night."

Sleet began to beat against the car. Deirdre squinted to keep an eye on the snow-covered road through the wipers scraping across the frosty windshield.

As the car approached a sharp curve, it skidded on the icy surface. She tapped on the brake pedal and turned the steering wheel trying to keep the car on the road but lost control. The car slid sideways, plowed through a broken guardrail, and plunged down a steep embankment. It crashed head-on into a large tree. The horn blared as the car came to an abrupt halt. The music played on eerily.

* * *

About an hour later, at home, Ben paced. He looked out the window. *Where is she?* He picked up the phone and called Deirdre's cell, but only got her voicemail. He then called Judy. "Jude, when did Deirdre leave there?"

"Geez, she left here over an hour ago. Why? Isn't she home yet?

"No, and I called her phone and she didn't answer. I'm starting to get worried. Real worried!"

"She might not try to answer her phone while driving. And maybe she just ran in to slow-moving traffic in this weather."

"Well, if she's not home soon, I'll start back-tracking to your house."

"Hopefully, she'll show up soon. Give me a call when she gets there. Okay?"

"Sure will."

Ben barely hung up the phone, when it rang. He answered. "Hello!" After listening to the person on the other end, he replied, "No! Oh my God! East Stroudsburg General? Thank you. I'll be right over." After hanging up, Ben immediately called Judy back. "Jude, I just got a call from the police. Deirdre's been in an accident. She's seriously injured. She's in the East Stroudsburg hospital. I'm going right over."

"Oh, no," Judy replied. "We'll meet you there. I'll call Penny. I'll call Julia and let her know, too. We'll pick both of them up on the way."

* * *

After sitting in a waiting room of the hospital for almost two hours, Ben leaned forward with elbows on his knees and shaky hands over his face. Justin hugged Judy while she rocked back and forth, her face white with anxiety. Penny and Julia sat still and stared straight ahead as if in a daze.

Ben stood up and ran his fingers through his hair. "God, it's been hours since we heard from any of those doctors." He paced back and forth, then sat back down.

Just then, a long-faced doctor came through the swinging door. Ben jumped up.

The doctor approached him. "Mr. Gardner, as I explained to you earlier, your wife suffered severe injuries, including a fractured skull and a punctured lung from broken ribs. She had massive internal bleeding. We did all we can. She's still alive, but—"

Ben collapsed back down into his chair, put his hand over his mouth and sobbed. The others began to weep.

"She's in intensive care," the doctor continued. "The nurse will show you there. I'll be there in a moment."

They shuffled into the intensive care room. Deirdre lay in the hospital bed. Monitors beeped. IV tubes protruded from her arms. Bandages covered the top of her head and one side of her face. Her left eye, nearly shut, swelled from her black and blue face.

They gathered around the bed. Ben reached down, took her hand and gently held on to it. Judy held her other hand.

Deirdre looked up with a faint smile and whispered, "I'm sorry, Ben. You always said I had a lead foot. Take care of Cody. He needs you. Someday we'll all be together again forever."

Ben bent over and gently kissed her cheek. "Now, don't talk like that. *We* will take care of Cody together at our house as soon as you get better. I love you, sweetheart. You're going to be okay." *Stay with us. Don't leave me. We need you.*

Penny moved closer to Judy and whispered. "It's not fair, Mom. Aunt Dee helped to save my life, and I can't help to save hers."

Deirdre appeared content and peaceful as her head turned slowly back and forth between Ben and Judy. She struggled to speak. Barely audible, she whispered. "It's okay. I'm okay now. Don't worry. I have a promise to keep."

She slowly closed her eyes and her body relaxed. The steady *beep, beep* of the heart monitor flatlined into a steady high-pitched tone. Ben and Judy backed away as a nurse, and then the doctor, rushed up to Deirdre. He slowly nodded, then shook his head.

Judy held on to Justin and burst into tears. Ben, feeling a sense of loss and grief that he couldn't bear, bit his hand, turned as if to punch the wall, but restrained himself.

Penny looked up with a startled look on her face. She pointed toward Deirdre and gasped. "L-L-look."

Ben stared as he stepped back from the bed. Judy looked at Penny, then toward Deirdre. Julia flopped down into a nearby chair, her mouth hanging open.

Deirdre's body took on a faint glow. The glow evolved into a wavy, cloud-like light. After levitating momentarily above her body, the wavy light floated upward.

Deirdre's physical body rested peacefully in the bed as the ghostly shape gradually rose from her. They all stared as the light faded and finally vanished.

Julia rose from the chair and turned to the others. "Something tells me Miss Dee will keep her promise. I think I know where her next stop is."

Chapter 41

Together Forever

DEIRDRE FOUND HERSELF standing in a meadow of colorful and fragrant flowers ... lilacs, roses, daffodils, and smiling daisies. It was exactly as Julia described. A light breeze blew across her hair. Above, a blue sky, sprinkled with shimmering shades of pink, spread endlessly over a landscape dotted with ponds and rolling hills of wispy grasses.

Trees of all sizes and varieties stood before her with lush, green leaves, many of them draped with apples, pears, mangos, bananas, nuts and other types of fruit. Small, clear brooks babbled, and waterfalls trickled. She knelt down and peered at her reflection in a calm pool. With hands raised, she slowly ran her fingers down across her face. She looked normal. Her hair dangled freely along the side of her face, showing no bruises, no marks, just the natural beauty she always had. She even wore her favorite T-shirt and shorts.

Barking dogs, meowing cats, and the sounds of other animals filled the air. Horses grazed in a lush green pasture, and a dog dashed by the brook.

Something warm and furry rubbed against her leg. She looked down. It was a cat. *Omigosh, it's Winky.* "Winky?"

She knelt to pet him, but he acted uninterested. Standing up, she looked down at him and nodded. "I know, Winky. You're waiting for Julia, aren't you?"

As Winky sprinted away, Deirdre continued to wander slowly through the lovely garden. Birds chirped. She stopped. One particular chirping sound stood out.

"Chirp, chirp, chirp."

While looking around, a beautiful green Fisher's lovebird with a bright red beak landed on her right shoulder. She smiled blissfully. "Timmy. You waited for me all this time. You look as beautiful as ever. My darling little Timmy."

Now realizing where she was, Deirdre felt a sense of intense euphoria. "Timmy, is Richard here? Did you see Richard? Oh, I wish you could tell me."

Standing still, Deirdre clasped her hands together and pressed them to her lips. She whispered with a soft, trembling voice, "Richard?" As she walked slowly among the trees, eyes darting from limb to limb, with cautious hope, she called in a louder voice, "Richard!" Stopping with head tilted, she heard nothing. Continuing to walk, she called out frantically, as loud as she could, "Richard!"

Walking at a faster pace, almost running, with her head rapidly turning side-to-side, she searched every tree, but no Richard. In despair, she fell to her knees and covered her face with her hands.

All at once, a childlike voice faintly called out from a distance. "Mommy!"

Deirdre raised her head and clutched at her chest. *Just my imagination.*

Again, this time louder, the voice called out. "Mommy! Mommy!"

With heightened senses and heart racing, Deirdre sprang to her feet and dashed in the direction of the voice. It became louder. "Mommy! Mommy!"

She stopped, held still in expectation, looked up, and grabbed at the sides of her head in elation.

There sat Richard in a tree, surrounded by small, pink and white apple blossoms. Spreading his wings, he spun in a circle and glided down to her outstretched arm. Bursting into happy tears, she pulled him close, hugged him, and smothered him with kisses.

"I love you, Mommy," Richard said.

"Oh, Richard, I love you too. And now we *are* going to be together again … in heaven."

With Richard on her left shoulder and Timmy on the other, she walked, with a feeling of weightlessness, through a sea of multicolored flowers that funneled toward a bright array of dazzling white lights. She gazed with wide, sparkling eyes, and a strange warmth radiated throughout her body. Mentally revisiting the hurdles leading to this moment, she turned to Richard and spoke softly. "Everything's okay now, Richard. Penny will live, and I'm going to take care of you forever, just like I promised."

Before her, a bridge, bordered by red, yellow, purple, and pink flowers, spanned over a white, fluffy cloud. The bridge surface, paved with golden bricks, dazzled in the sunlight. Seven arching rainbows glittered and lined each side of the bridge. Above, one enormous rainbow shimmered brightly and hovered over the entire bridge. On the other side of the bridge, a bright shining light twinkled and emanated outward like slow-motion fireworks.

A force drew Deirdre toward the light.

She turned to Richard. "Richard, Julia was right. It really does exist. This is it ... the Rainbow Bridge. And some day Ben and Cody will join us on the other side. Then we'll all be together again."

Timmy chirped.

Richard turned his head toward the bridge. "Pretty, pretty."

With a feeling of being at total peace, Deirdre, with Richard on one shoulder and Timmy on the other, walked calmly across the Rainbow Bridge.

A white mist gradually surrounded them, and together, they disappeared into the bright light.

Epilogue

SUNLIGHT BEAMED through the window by Cody's cage. Ben sat in a nearby chair gazing at photos of Deirdre, Richard, and Timmy. Glancing over at an end table, he noticed an unopened envelope addressed to Deirdre. The return address read, Child Smile Publishing. He opened it and started reading.

Dear Ms. Gardner,

We are pleased to inform you that we accept for publication your most recent book, "Richard's Adventures." Our entire staff is excited by the possibilities of this literature project.

Find enclosed with this letter of approval—

Ben lowered the letter to his lap, and his eyes teared up. He couldn't bear to read on. *Oh, how hard she worked on that book about Richard.* He thought about how excited she was when she got a letter from her publisher years ago. He remembered that day clearly … how she rushed to him wearing her favorite T-shirt that read, Standing Strong Against Childhood Cancer, playfully holding a letter behind her back, bouncing on her toes … how she kissed him, eyes shining, smiling from ear to ear … how she wanted him to go to New York with her. God, how he missed her spontaneity, her beautiful mind and spirit. *I should have told her more how much I loved her.* Ben turned toward Cody. "You know, old friend, I feel like I lost a part of myself. Tomorrow is never guaranteed for anyone."

Cody squawked.

Ben lowered the photos, stood up, took Cody out of the cage, and sat down again. Cody dropped his head, indicating he wanted Ben to scratch it. Ben's chin trembled as he ran his fingers through Cody's feathers.

"I know you miss them too, Cody," Ben said as his throat thickened. "Dee and Richard and Timmy sure changed our lives. Come to think of it, if it hadn't been for you and Timmy, Dee would have never had any reason to go to Woody's Bird Farm. She wouldn't have met Richard. And Penny would have died. Gosh, it just occurred to me … the *Amazon* rainforest passed on the gift of healing to Dee's *Amazon* parrot. It truly was the *gift of the Amazon*!"

As if aware of Ben's feelings, Cody cocked his head and looked directly into Ben's eyes.

"Yes, Cody, Dee and Richard certainly made a believer out of me. There are just some things that can't be explained through science. Something tells me we'll be with them again someday." Ben picked up a photo of Deirdre with Richard perched on her shoulder, lowered it, looked up at the ceiling, and sighed. "I love you, Dee, and you too, Richard and Timmy."

Ben got up and put Cody back into his cage. Returning to his chair, he leaned back for a moment, folded his hands behind his head, and stared into empty space. Visions of the Cinta Larga Indian village deep within the Amazon rainforest flashed through his mind. *I wonder what's happening there. How will the Indians ever get along without Dr. Ryman?*

* * *

In the Brazilian rainforest, a handsome, now teenaged Tiko, sprinted along a trail. Deirdre's rawhide butterfly necklace hung from his neck. He stopped at the tall kapok tree with the hollow in the trunk. As he looked up and extended his arm, the rawhide bracelet with the two familiar charms, one in the shape of a butterfly, the other shaped like three twisted prongs, dangled from his wrist.

A beautiful Blue-fronted Amazon parrot emerged from the hollow. The mostly green parrot had yellow feathering around his eyes and yellow and red blotches on the shoulders of his wings. His most outstanding feature, the striking turquoise-blue color on his forehead, glistened in the sunlight filtering through the rainforest. He spread his wings revealing the mark of a white butterfly on the side of his body and glided down to Tiko's outstretched hand.

"My little one," Tiko said, "you are no longer the baby papagaio I first see in the kapok. We grow together. You and I ... we are one. We have much to do. I will be back." Tiko kissed his friend gently, raised his arm, and the parrot flapped his wings as he ascended into the jungle sky.

Tiko smiled and sauntered back down the trail so many of his ancestors had walked before him. The jungle mist enshrouded the young man, and a white birthmark in the shape of a butterfly on the back of his shoulder glistened in the sunlight.

As Tiko disappeared down the path, a white dove sat quietly above on a nearby tree branch.

About the Authors

Barry and Darlene Greenawald are a happily retired couple living in The Villages, Florida. Barry was a biologist with the Pennsylvania Department of Environmental Protection for 36 years. Darlene started her career as an English teacher in upstate New York and held purchasing and contracting positions in Pennsylvania local and state agencies.

Authors' Note

The Blue-fronted Amazon parrot in this story really does exist and has filled our lives with many wonderful moments. As of the writing of this book, our parrot was twenty-two years old.

He does say or has said all the words and phrases contained in the story, and he actually has done many of the activities mentioned in the story, including turning a nut with his beak.

It is the real-life, close bond between Darlene and this parrot that first inspired Barry to write this story as a feature film screenplay. To expand the story, and to broaden its exposure, Darlene and Barry collaborated to turn the screenplay into this book.

Questions and Topics for Discussion

1. Deirdre has a very special bond with a parrot. Have you ever had a pet that you felt an amazing connection to?

2. People underestimate the intelligence and emotions of animals in general. Can you think of any specifics where animals have shown the power to reason and make decisions in their response to a situation?

3. When animals speak, they take on a whole different dimension. If your animal could speak, what do you think he/she would say to you?

4. What do you think is the significance of the appearance of the white dove at crucial time periods in the story?

5. Why do you think the Cinta Larga Indians felt it was important to keep Ubjara's bracelet instead of burying it with him?

6. The destruction of the Amazon rainforest has been a topic of much discussion. What are your feelings regarding the deforestation and mining operations that have been done in that area? How have they affected the people who live there and the world in general?

7. What was your reaction to Reverend James? Can you name others in real life that may parallel this antagonist?

8. If you had to use one word to describe Deirdre, what would it be and why?

9. Have you ever made a promise to someone? What lengths did you go through to make sure you kept your promise?

10. Throughout the novel, the characters find themselves in some difficult situations. Is there one that you found more exciting or memorable than the others?

11. Deirdre's T-shirt said, Standing Strong Against Childhood Cancer. What cause would you support and what would your T-shirt say and why?

12. We all have fears and phobias in real life. Deirdre's was claustrophobia; Ben's was fear of water. What are your fears and how do you deal with them?

Made in the USA
Columbia, SC
26 November 2017